INFINITE POTENTIAL LEADERSHIP

Unlocking Boundless Growth and Transformational Leadership

Joel R. Klemmer

encouraged to consider the information as guidance and should not interpret it as a promise or guarantee of specific outcomes.

Content Accuracy Disclaimer: While every effort has been made to ensure the accuracy and reliability of the content in this book, errors, omissions, or inaccuracies may exist. Readers are advised to use their discretion and verify information independently when necessary. The author and publisher do not assume responsibility for any consequences, losses, or damages resulting from reliance on the information presented herein.

Content Sensitivity Disclaimer: This book may contain discussions on sensitive or potentially triggering topics. Readers are advised to be aware of the nature of the content and exercise discretion when reading. It is essential to take necessary precautions and seek appropriate support or guidance if you find any content distressing or challenging. The author acknowledges the potential sensitivity of these topics and encourages readers to prioritize their emotional well-being.

Endorsement Disclaimer: Mention of products, services, organizations, or other entities in this book is for illustrative purposes only. It does not constitute an endorsement, recommendation, or affiliation with these entities. The author and publisher have no formal association with the mentioned products, services, or organizations, and the content should not be interpreted as an endorsement or sponsorship of any kind. Readers should conduct their research and assessments independently when considering such entities or offerings.

First Edition: 2024

To the courageous leaders, thinkers, and dreamers—

This book is dedicated to you.

To those who dare to embrace the journey of growth, who see potential where others see limitations, and who commit themselves to empowering not only their teams but also themselves. You are the ones who challenge the status quo, push beyond the boundaries of the possible, and inspire others to do the same.

To the readers who not only absorb knowledge but apply it in their everyday lives, both in their professional roles and personal relationships. This book is for those who understand that leadership is a continuous evolution, a path filled with learning, and a mission to leave the world better than you found it.

Thank you for your dedication to growth, transformation, and unlocking the infinite potential within yourselves and those around you. It is your vision, resilience, and commitment to making a lasting impact that will shape a brighter, more innovative future.

May these pages serve as a guide, a source of inspiration, and a reminder that your leadership journey is one of limitless possibilities.

With gratitude and admiration,

This book is for you.

Table of Contents

Introduction
The Dawn of a New Leadership Era

At the core of great leadership lies a powerful truth: every individual, every team, and every organization possesses an untapped well of potential. This potential is not limited by past achievements or the constraints of present circumstances; it is boundless, ever-evolving, and capable of creating extraordinary outcomes. The concept of Infinite Potential Leadership challenges the traditional view that leaders are defined by their personal abilities or singular vision. Instead, it invites us to see leadership as a dynamic process of unlocking growth in others, harnessing the collective talents and capacities of those we lead, and embracing the belief that the future holds limitless possibilities.

In this framework, leadership is not merely about achieving short-term goals or managing resources efficiently but about creating an environment where continuous learning, innovation, and personal development thrive. It is about understanding that potential is not a fixed quantity—there is always more to discover, more to create, and more to become.

In the rapidly changing landscape of today's world, where technological advancements, global challenges, and societal shifts are happening at unprecedented rates, leaders must adapt their thinking. They can no longer rely solely on what worked in the past. Instead, they must cultivate a mindset that sees beyond limitations—both in themselves and their organizations. This is the essence of infinite potential leadership: the belief that growth is a constant and that by fostering this belief in themselves and their teams, leaders can unlock extraordinary levels of creativity, resilience, and achievement.

Imagine the possibilities if you, as a leader, viewed every challenge as an opportunity to expand, every setback as a chance to innovate, and every person around you as capable of far more than they realize. When leaders adopt this perspective, they transcend the ordinary and step into the role of catalysts for transformation—not just within their organizations but within society at large. This is not a lofty ideal but a practical approach to leadership that harnesses the very nature of human capacity.

The journey to becoming a leader of infinite potential begins with a shift in how we see our role. It requires moving away from the idea that leadership is about personal power or control and toward realizing that true leadership is about cultivating the boundless potential that exists in others. When leaders embrace this mindset, they not only elevate their own leadership but also ignite a never-ending chain reaction of growth and possibility within their teams and organizations.

As we explore how leaders can activate this infinite potential, tapping into a deeper well of creativity, vision, and impact altogether, we will uncover the tools and strategies needed to break through limitations and the ability to lead in a way that inspires continuous growth and transformation—both, for ourselves and those we lead.

For decades, traditional leadership models were the basis of organizational success. These models – often built on hierarchical structures, clear chains of command, and a focus on efficiency and control – played a critical role in stabilizing organizations and driving them forward in relatively predictable environments. Leaders were expected to be the ultimate decision-makers, directing teams toward established goals with a firm hand and a well-defined strategy.

While this approach worked quite effectively in the past, it is essential to note that today's world has changed dramatically. The pace of technological advancement, the complexity of global markets, and the rise of remote workforces have created an environment far more dynamic, uncertain, and interconnected than ever before. In this new landscape, the traditional models of leadership—rooted in fixed authority, rigid structures, and singular decision-making—are struggling to keep up.

One of the main reasons traditional leadership is no longer sufficient is its inability to respond effectively to rapid change. Today's challenges require leaders to be agile, adaptive, and open to continuous learning. On the contrary, many traditional models mainly emphasize maintaining control and following established processes. In a world where disruptions can occur overnight—whether from new technologies, shifting consumer demands, or global crises—leaders must be equipped to pivot, innovate, and respond flexibly. Rigid adherence to old ways of thinking can leave organizations vulnerable, hindering their capability to react promptly.

Moreover, the command-and-control leadership style, where power is concentrated at the top, often stifles the creativity and innovation necessary for modern success. In a world where knowledge and expertise are more distributed than ever, organizations thrive only when leadership is shared, collaboration is encouraged, and employees at all levels are empowered to contribute. Yet, many traditional models discourage this kind of decentralized leadership, limiting the flow of ideas and underutilizing the potential of teams.

On the other side of the light, the expectations of today's workforce have evolved. Employees now seek more than just a paycheck; they want purpose, autonomy, and opportunities for personal growth. The top-down leadership approach, which focuses on direction and oversight, often fails to engage the modern worker meaningfully. In contrast, leaders who recognize the infinite potential within their teams can inspire greater loyalty, creativity, and drive by creating environments where people feel valued, challenged, and capable of achieving more than they thought possible.

Finally, traditional leadership models tend to prioritize short-term results over long-term growth. In today's complex and interconnected world, leaders must take a more holistic view, understanding that success is no longer defined solely by quarterly profits or efficiency metrics. Instead, leaders must broaden their perspective to see the bigger picture—one that includes sustainability, social impact, and the well-being of their teams. This requires a shift from transactional leadership, which focuses on immediate returns, to transformational leadership, which seeks to unlock potential and create lasting change.

While traditional leadership models were once effective in a more stable and predictable world, they are inadequate in today's fast-moving, interconnected environment. The challenges and opportunities leaders face now require a different approach—one that is more agile, inclusive, and growth-oriented. To thrive in this dynamic world, leaders must move beyond the limitations of the past and embrace new models of leadership that recognize and cultivate the infinite potential within themselves, their teams, and their organizations.

At the heart of the Infinite Potential Leadership lies a simple yet profound belief: that leaders, organizations, and the systems they inhabit have within them an untapped and limitless potential for growth and transformation. Unlike traditional leadership models, which often view potential as a finite resource-constrained by existing abilities, resources, or circumstances, this theory challenges those assumptions. It invites us to see leadership as a dynamic, evolving process where growth knows no boundaries. In this framework, leadership becomes less about managing limitations and more about expanding possibilities.

The journey of infinite potential begins with the leader. Every individual, regardless of their past experiences or current status, holds within themselves an infinite capacity for personal development, creativity, and impact. Under this theory, leadership is not a static achievement or a title—it is an ongoing, ever-evolving journey. Leaders are not defined by their past successes or constrained by their current skills. Instead, they have the power to evolve, learn, and reinvent themselves continuously. This continuous growth is the cornerstone of their ability to lead in a world that demands constant adaptation.

Think about the leaders who have transformed industries or inspired social movements. They did not settle into their roles and stop growing; instead, they relentlessly pursued new knowledge, skills, and perspectives. They understood that to be an effective leader is to be a lifelong learner, constantly expanding their vision, capabilities, and understanding of the world around them. These leaders did not view themselves as finished products but rather as works in progress—always growing, always transforming, and always capable of achieving more. This is the mindset of infinite potential in leadership: the recognition that no matter how far you have come, there is always more to discover, more to create, and more to become.

However, this idea of infinite potential does not stop with the individual leader. Organizations, too, possess this same limitless potential for growth and transformation. Organizations are not fixed entities; they are living systems capable of evolving in response to their environments, opportunities, and challenges. Whether through innovation, cultural shifts, or strategic pivots, organizations have the capacity to reinvent themselves and reach new heights of success. The key is to recognize that potential is not just 'something' that diminishes over time or is constrained by current conditions; instead, it is the wealth that can be cultivated and expanded indefinitely.

Consider the countless companies that have transformed their industries—organizations that refused to accept the status quo and instead chose to see their own potential as limitless. These organizations embraced change, fostered a culture of innovation, and continuously sought ways to improve and evolve. They did not rest on their laurels or become complacent with their past successes; they understood that the only constant in the world is change and that to thrive, they must be willing to evolve with it. This willingness to embrace change to challenge the limits of what is possible is what allows organizations to unlock their infinite potential.

The Infinite Potential Leadership also extends beyond the individual leader and the organization to encompass the broader systems in which they operate. Industries, economies, and even societal structures are not static entities; they are interconnected systems that are constantly evolving. Leaders and organizations are parts of these larger systems, and their actions have ripple effects that influence the entire network. When leaders recognize this interconnectedness, they begin to understand that their capacity for influence and change is far greater than they ever imagined. The system itself holds infinite potential, and it enables the leaders to harness that potential to drive transformation not just within their organizations but across the entire set of industries and communities.

This idea of infinite potential is closely tied to the concept of systems thinking. Leaders who adopt a system-based approach understand that their actions and decisions do not exist in a vacuum. Every choice they make has consequences that extend beyond the immediate team or organization, influencing the broader system of stakeholders, partners, and even society at large. When leaders approach leadership with this holistic view, they get the ability to see how their actions contribute to a larger tapestry of change, allowing them to harness the power of interconnectedness to achieve far-reaching results.

In this way, leaders and organizations that embrace the Infinite Potential Leadership embrace the potential to become catalysts for global change. They are not merely focused on their own success; they see themselves as part of a larger, interconnected web of possibilities. They recognize that by unlocking the infinite potential within their own spheres of influence. They can drive positive transformation that reverberates across the world. This is the kind of leadership that inspires global movements, advances industries, and shapes the future.

Central to unlocking infinite potential is a mindset shift—a fundamental change in how leaders and organizations view their roles and capacities. Traditionally, leadership has often been framed within a paradigm of limitations: limited resources, limited time, and limited growth opportunities. The Infinite Potential Leadership turns this perspective on its head. It challenges the belief that growth has a ceiling or that success is finite. On the contrary, it proposes that leadership is about continuously pushing beyond perceived boundaries and cultivating the limitless capacity for growth in oneself and others.

To fully embrace infinite potential, leaders must adopt a mindset of abundance rather than scarcity. This means seeing possibilities where others see constraints and viewing every challenge as an opportunity for further growth and innovation instead of focusing on what cannot be done. Leaders who embrace infinite potential focus on what can be done, constantly seeking new ways to unlock creativity and potential in their teams and organizations. This shift from a scarcity mindset to one of abundance is critical in transforming how leaders approach problems, develop strategies, and inspire those around them.

Moreover, this shift requires leaders to move from a mindset of control to that of empowerment. In traditional leadership models, leaders often feel the need to control every decision, every process, and every outcome. But in a world of infinite potential, leaders recognize that true power comes not from control but from empowering others. By creating an environment where team members feel supported, valued, and encouraged to explore their own potential, leaders unlock a cascade of growth that extends far beyond what any individual could achieve alone.

In essence, Infinite Potential Leadership is about seeing leadership as a journey of endless possibility, perceiving it as means, not mere ends, as imparted by the traditional view. It invites leaders to expand their vision of what is possible, to recognize the boundless potential within themselves and their organizations, and to embrace the interconnectedness of the systems in which they operate. In doing so, they unlock not just incremental growth but transformational change—a change that has the power to shape industries, communities, and the world.

At the heart of the Infinite Potential Leadership are ten essential dimensions that represent the building blocks of great leadership. These dimensions are more than just qualities or skills—they are interconnected aspects of leadership that work together to help leaders realize their full potential and that of their organizations. Each dimension plays a crucial role in shaping how leaders navigate challenges, inspire others, and create meaningful, lasting change. Together, they form a roadmap for unlocking the boundless growth that lies within every leader, team, and organization.

The first dimension is Vision. Great leaders are defined by their ability to see beyond the immediate and imagine a future filled with possibility. Vision is not just about setting goals; it is about painting a picture of a future that inspires others to believe in something bigger than themselves. A leader with vision provides direction, a sense of purpose, and a compelling reason for people to invest their energy and creativity in achieving shared goals. Vision is the cornerstone of transformative leadership—it shows the way forward, even when the path is unclear.

Next is Wisdom, a dimension that speaks to the leader's ability to balance intuition with rational thought. In an increasingly complex world, leaders must be able to make decisions that consider both immediate realities and long-term consequences. Wisdom is what enables leaders to navigate uncertainty with clarity. It is not just about having knowledge; it is about knowing how and when to apply it. Leaders who cultivate wisdom are able to perceive patterns, understand the deeper implications of their choices, and guide their organizations through complexity with confidence and foresight.

Understanding is the third dimension, vital for creating deep connections with others. Great leaders are not only aware of their own strengths and weaknesses but are also highly attuned to the needs, motivations, and perspectives of those they lead. This understanding fosters trust and collaboration, allowing leaders to meet people where they are and guide them toward collective success. When leaders genuinely understand their teams, they can unlock hidden potential, address challenges effectively, and inspire loyalty and dedication.

The fourth dimension, Compassion, is what transforms leadership from a task of management to a journey of human connection. Compassionate leaders lead with empathy, genuinely caring for the well-being of those around them. They create environments where people feel supported, valued, and empowered to grow. Compassion does not mean being unnecessarily lenient or avoiding difficult decisions; rather, it involves balancing care with accountability, ensuring that people have the space and support they need to achieve their best while being held to high standards. Leaders who lead with compassion create cultures of trust, loyalty, and growth.

Discipline is the fifth dimension, and it is the quality that turns vision into reality. Without discipline, even the most inspiring visions can falter. Discipline is about staying focused, setting clear boundaries, and consistently following through on commitments. It allows leaders to execute their plans with precision and hold themselves and others accountable for results. Discipline is not about rigidity but rather about consistency and the willingness to make the tough choices necessary to achieve long-term success.

The sixth dimension is Harmony, which reflects a leader's ability to balance competing priorities and integrate diverse perspectives. In any leadership role, conflicting ideas and needs will arise. Leaders who can harmonize these differences, rather than allowing them to create division, are able to bring people together in pursuit of common goals. Harmony is about finding balance—between short-term and long-term needs, between individual ambitions and collective success, and between different viewpoints within a team. Leaders who master this dimension create environments of collaboration and unity where the strength of the group is greater than the sum of its parts.

Resilience is the seventh dimension; in today's fast-changing world, it is more important than ever. Resilient leaders can navigate adversity, bounce back from setbacks, and remain steady in the face of uncertainty. Resilience is not about avoiding failure; it is about learning from it and coming back stronger. Leaders who cultivate resilience inspire confidence in their teams, showing them that challenges are not roadblocks but opportunities for growth. This dimension allows leaders to weather storms and keep their organizations moving forward, regardless of all odds and obstacles.

The eighth dimension, Humility, is perhaps one of the most underrated qualities of leadership, yet it is essential for sustainable success. Humility allows leaders to recognize that they do not have all the answers and that they can learn from others. Humble leaders are open to feedback, willing to admit mistakes, and constantly striving to improve. This openness fosters a learning culture within the organization, where people feel safe to innovate, experiment, and grow. Humility is not about diminishing one's achievements but about leading with a grounded sense of self, knowing that the success of the organization is a collective effort.

Integrity, the ninth dimension, is the foundation of trust. Leaders with integrity are consistent in aligning their actions with their values. They are transparent, honest, and ethical in their decision-making, which builds a strong culture of trust within the organization. Integrity is what allows leaders to inspire confidence—not just in their abilities but in their character. In a world where ethical leadership is more important than ever, leaders with integrity are able to build long-term, sustainable success that extends beyond profit margins to create meaningful impact.

Finally, the tenth dimension is Stewardship, which reflects the idea that leadership is about service. Stewardship is recognizing that leaders are caretakers of the people, resources, and missions entrusted to them. Great leaders understand that their role is not just to achieve short-term results but to nurture long-term success for the organization and its people. Stewardship is about creating a legacy that benefits others, ensuring that the actions taken today set the foundation for future growth and sustainability.

These ten dimensions of leadership—vision, wisdom, understanding, compassion, discipline, harmony, resilience, humility, integrity, and stewardship—form the core of the Infinite Potential Leadership. Each dimension is essential for unlocking the boundless potential that exists within leaders and their organizations. Together, they provide a comprehensive roadmap for leadership that is not just about managing what already exists but about expanding into what it could become. By cultivating these dimensions, leaders can inspire continuous growth, foster transformative change, and create lasting impact in their organizations and beyond.

Chapter 1
The Infinite Potential Within

I Imagine, for a moment, what it would feel like to live in a world where the concept of limits does not exist. Where instead of being constrained by what is immediately possible, every person, every idea, and every endeavor is imbued with the potential for endless growth. In this world, there are no ceilings to what can be achieved—only an ever-expanding horizon of possibilities. This is the world that great leaders must learn to see because this is the world of infinite potential.

At the foundation of Infinite Potential Leadership is the belief that every individual, team, and organization holds within them the boundless capacity for growth, innovation, and transformation. It is not just a motivational idea but a fundamental shift in how we perceive ourselves and those around us. Leadership, from this perspective, is not about merely managing resources or achieving short-term results; it's about tapping into the limitless possibilities that lie within people and systems and inspiring them to achieve far beyond their perceived limits.

For centuries, traditional leadership has been built around the idea of managing the known and seen—resources, people, processes, and time—within a limited framework. But in today's world, this approach is no longer sufficient. The challenges we face, from technological advancements to global complexities, demand more from leaders than ever before. What worked in the past—managing limitations and staying within known boundaries—will not suffice to lead us into the future. Instead, leaders must cultivate a mindset of infinite potential, one that sees beyond current circumstances and recognizes that growth is not finite. It is limitless.

Recognizing limitless growth in ourselves and others is essential for leadership in today's dynamic, fast-paced world because the nature of leadership itself has changed. No longer are leaders expected to simply direct and control; instead, they are called upon to inspire, cultivate creativity, and unlock the hidden potential within their teams and organizations. This requires a different kind of thinking—a belief that people are not static, that organizations are not defined by their current structure, and that success is not capped by what has already been achieved.

Consider the most transformative leaders throughout history—those who have not just managed change but have created it. They were not limited by what was seen as "possible" at the time. Instead, they believed in something more, something greater. They saw potential in situations where others saw limitations. Leaders like Martin Luther King Jr., who envisioned a future of equality when the present was defined by division. Leaders like Steve Jobs, who imagined a world where technology could be simple, accessible, and personal when others thought computers were for experts only. What set these leaders apart was their ability to see beyond the current reality and tap into the infinite potential that lies in the human spirit.

This mindset is crucial in today's world because the pace of change is unprecedented. New technologies emerge daily, global challenges require new solutions, and the expectations of the modern workforce are evolving rapidly. Leaders can no longer afford to think in terms of fixed resources or limited growth. Instead, they must recognize that their most valuable asset is the potential of their people—their capacity to learn, adapt, innovate, and create. When leaders understand that potential is not a finite resource, they stop limiting themselves and their teams to what is already known or already achieved.

In practical terms, recognizing infinite potential means leading with a belief that every person has the capacity to grow, contribute in new ways, and surpass expectations. It means creating environments where people are not just allowed but encouraged to explore their talents, expand their skills, and stretch beyond what they thought possible. This kind of leadership benefits not only the individual but also the entire organization at large. When people believe that their potential is limitless, they become more engaged, more creative, and more willing to take the risks necessary for innovation and progress.

For leaders, this mindset also requires self-awareness. Recognizing the infinite potential in others begins with recognizing it in yourself. Leaders must be willing to challenge their own limits and commit to continuous learning and evolution. Leadership is not a fixed state—it is a journey of personal growth. The best leaders understand that they, too, are capable of more than they initially imagined. They lead by example, showing their teams that growth is a never-ending process and that there is always more to learn, more to achieve, and more to become.

This belief in infinite potential changes the way leaders approach challenges. Instead of seeing obstacles as insurmountable barriers, they view them as opportunities for growth. Leaders who embrace this mindset are not afraid of failure because they understand that every setback is simply another chance to learn and grow. This resilience is essential in today's world, where uncertainty is the norm and adaptability is the key to survival. Leaders who recognize their own limitless potential are better equipped to guide their teams through challenges with confidence and optimism.

Moreover, the idea of infinite potential extends beyond the individual and the organization to encompass entire systems. In today's interconnected world, leaders must think holistically, understanding that their decisions impact not just their teams but the larger ecosystems of which they are a part. This requires a broader vision, one that sees potential in the interconnectedness of people, organizations, and communities. Leaders who embrace this perspective can drive change that goes beyond immediate results, creating lasting, transformative impact.

Ultimately, the foundation of infinite potential is about believing in the power of possibility. It is about recognizing that the future is not limited by the past and that growth is not constrained by current circumstances. Leaders who cultivate this mindset are able to unlock extraordinary levels of creativity, resilience, and innovation within themselves and those they lead. They understand that leadership is not about controlling outcomes but about creating environments where people can thrive and reach their fullest potential.

Throughout history, certain leaders have transcended the boundaries of conventional thinking, reshaping industries, cultures, and even nations. What unites these transformative figures is their shared belief in boundless potential—the idea that neither they nor the people they led are constrained by present circumstances. They imagined a future beyond immediate limitations, and through their leadership, they unlocked growth not just for themselves but for their organizations and societies as a whole.

Nelson Mandela's journey of boundless leadership growth began in the most confined of places: a prison cell. Sentenced to life imprisonment for his fight against South Africa's apartheid regime, Mandela spent 27 years in jail. Many would believe that kind of prolonged confinement would lead to anger or resignation. But Mandela saw the potential for transformation not just in himself but in his entire country. Instead of emerging from prison consumed by bitterness, he chose a path of reconciliation and unity. Mandela understood that South Africa's future could only be secured through forgiveness and not revenge.

His leadership was not about immediate victories but about laying the foundation for long-term healing and growth. He saw the boundless potential in a divided nation, one that could emerge stronger and more united after years of racial segregation. Mandela's belief in the limitless potential for peace and understanding led to the dismantling of apartheid and the creation of a democratic South Africa. His legacy is not just political; it is deeply human. He demonstrated that real growth begins within and radiates outward, inspiring a nation—and the world—to believe in the power of reconciliation.

When Satya Nadella became CEO of Microsoft in 2014, many saw the company as a relic of its former self. The once-dominant tech giant was losing its innovative edge, having fallen behind in areas like mobile computing and cloud technology. Nadella, however, saw Microsoft's potential not as a thing of the past but as something boundless and ripe for reinvention. Rather than focusing solely on financial metrics or technological catch-up, Nadella introduced a new philosophy: the growth mindset.

He encouraged employees at every level of Microsoft to embrace a culture of learning, experimentation, and failure as a path to innovation. Under his leadership, Microsoft shifted its focus to the cloud and artificial intelligence, positioning itself as a leader in the future of technology. More importantly, Nadella redefined the company's culture—turning it from a competitive, inward-looking environment into one that celebrated collaboration and inclusivity. By believing in the boundless potential of his employees and the company's ability to evolve, Nadella transformed Microsoft into one of the most valuable and innovative companies in the world.

Few stories exemplify boundless personal growth as much as that of Sara Blakely, the founder of Spanx. With no formal background in fashion, business, or design, Blakely started her company with $5,000 in savings and a vision to revolutionize women's shapewear. In the late 1990s, the industry was dominated by uncomfortable products, far from flattering. Most would have seen this as a market too challenging to penetrate, but Blakely saw it as an opportunity.

Blakely's belief in her own potential—and her refusal to accept limitations—led her to create an entirely new category of shapewear. From cold-calling factories to persuading department stores to stock her product, she pushed through every obstacle with relentless optimism. Spanx became a billion-dollar brand, not only revolutionizing women's undergarments but also setting new standards for female entrepreneurship. Blakely's journey is a testament to the power of believing in boundless potential. She did not just build a product; she built an empire rooted in her ability to push beyond her own limitations.

If there is one leader today who embodies the concept of boundless potential, it is Elon Musk. Musk's ventures—from Tesla to SpaceX—are driven by his belief in limitless possibilities. Where others see obstacles, Musk sees opportunities for growth and innovation. When Tesla was in its infancy, many doubted the feasibility of a company dedicated to electric vehicles. The automotive industry was deeply entrenched in gasoline-powered cars, and many saw the shift to sustainable energy as too costly and too difficult to achieve on a large scale. Musk, however, saw a future where electric cars were not only viable but would revolutionize the automotive industry.

Likewise, with SpaceX, Musk pursued the audacious goal of reducing space travel costs and ultimately colonizing Mars. To most, these aspirations seemed more like science fiction than a business plan. Yet, by believing in the boundless potential of technology and human ingenuity, Musk has not only turned SpaceX into a leader in the space industry but has also reignited global interest in space exploration. His leadership philosophy is simple: never be constrained by what seems possible today. Always push for what could be possible tomorrow.

Oprah Winfrey's story is one of overcoming tremendous adversity to become one of the world's most powerful media figures. Born into poverty and raised in a society that did not expect much from women of color, Oprah faced obstacles at every turn. Yet, she never allowed these challenges to limit her vision of what she could achieve. Oprah believed deeply in her own potential and worked relentlessly to expand it. What started as a small talk show became a media empire, and Oprah used her platform not just to entertain but to inspire millions.

Her belief in the boundless potential of others has been a defining characteristic of her leadership. Through her television shows, book club, and philanthropic efforts, Oprah has consistently sought to uplift and empower those around her. She exemplifies the idea that when leaders believe in their own growth and the growth of others, the ripple effects can transform lives on a global scale.

Howard Schultz, the former CEO of Starbucks, is another leader who believed in boundless growth—not just for his company but for the communities it served. Schultz grew up in public housing in Brooklyn, and his early life experiences shaped his belief that businesses have a responsibility to do more than just make a profit. Under his leadership, Starbucks did not just expand its global footprint; it redefined what a corporation could be by focusing on values and purpose.

Schultz introduced benefits like healthcare for part-time employees, stock options, and support for ethical sourcing practices. He saw the potential for Starbucks to become not just a coffee company but a force for good in the world. His leadership was driven by the idea that businesses, too, have boundless potential—not just in terms of financial growth but in their ability to create positive social impact.

As the CEO of PepsiCo, Indra Nooyi took on the challenge of leading one of the world's largest companies into the future. Rather than focusing solely on profit, Nooyi believed in the potential for PepsiCo to lead the way in creating healthier, more sustainable products. She introduced the concept of "Performance with Purpose," balancing financial success with social responsibility. Nooyi saw PepsiCo's potential not just as a snack and beverage giant but as a company that could make a positive impact on health and sustainability globally.

Her leadership was grounded in the belief that even large, established corporations have room for transformation and growth. By embracing innovation and challenging the status quo, Nooyi led PepsiCo to achieve strong financial performance while also reducing its environmental impact and expanding its portfolio of healthier products. Her belief in the boundless potential for growth—both in business and social responsibility—set a new standard for corporate leadership.

Jeff Bezos, the founder of Amazon, has long been driven by a belief in boundless potential. From its beginnings as an online bookstore, Bezos envisioned Amazon as something much larger—a platform that could offer nearly every product imaginable, powered by continuous innovation. His philosophy of "Day 1 thinking" embodies the idea that growth and innovation should never stop, no matter how successful the company becomes.

Under Bezos's leadership, Amazon grew from a simple e-commerce platform into a global powerhouse that disrupted industries from retail to cloud computing. Bezos's ability to see beyond current limitations and relentlessly pursue new opportunities has made Amazon one of the most influential companies in the world. His leadership demonstrates that when leaders embrace boundless growth, they can transform not only their organizations but entire industries.

What unites these leaders—Mandela, Nadella, Blakely, Musk, Oprah, Schultz, Nooyi, and Bezos—is their shared belief in boundless potential. They did not allow themselves or their organizations to be limited by current circumstances or conventional thinking. Instead, they pushed beyond perceived limitations, unlocking new possibilities for growth and transformation. Their stories remind us that leadership is not about managing what exists—it is about imagining what it could become and taking bold steps to turn that vision into reality. These leaders demonstrate that believing in the infinite potential within oneself can set absolutely no limits to whatever one can achieve.

Infinite Potential Leadership is a fundamental shift in mindset—one that moves away from a focus on limitations and scarcity and toward a belief in boundless possibilities. This mindset shift is transformative not only in the way leaders see themselves but also in how they view their teams, organizations, and the challenges they face. When leaders adopt a mindset of infinite possibilities, they unlock new approaches to problem-solving, innovation, and growth. It is this shift that enables them to transcend the constraints of the present and lead their organizations into the future.

Leadership, as traditionally understood, often revolves around managing resources: time, talent, finances, and knowledge. Leaders are taught to make decisions based on what is available to them in the moment, which can often result in a narrow focus on short-term solutions and incremental growth. In this framework, leadership is seen as a balancing act—managing competing interests and maximizing what is possible within existing constraints. However, when a leader embraces a mindset of infinite possibilities, this balancing act becomes something far more dynamic and exciting. Rather than managing limits, leaders begin to focus on expanding them.

A leader professing infinite possibilities approaches every challenge not as a barrier but as an opportunity to unlock new growth. This perspective shift changes the nature of leadership itself. Instead of seeing obstacles as fixed, these leaders recognize that obstacles are simply steppingstones toward greater innovation and creativity. Where others might see a dead end, they see potential—potential to grow, to learn, and to find solutions that have not been tried before.

Consider how this mindset shift worked out in the leadership of Elon Musk. When Musk first envisioned Tesla, he did not see the entrenched dominance of gasoline-powered cars as an insurmountable obstacle. He saw it as a challenge that could be overcome by pushing the boundaries of what was possible with electric vehicle technology. The automotive industry was not structured to support the widespread adoption of electric cars. Infrastructure was lacking, public interest was low, and skeptics abounded. However, Musk's mindset was not rooted in what currently existed; it was focused on what could exist. This belief in infinite possibilities allowed him to build a company that not only created electric vehicles but sparked a global shift in how we think about sustainable transportation.

Similarly, in the realm of organizational leadership, Satya Nadella's transformation of Microsoft is a clear example of how a mindset of infinite possibilities can reshape an entire company. When Nadella took over as CEO, Microsoft had lost much of its competitive edge. The company was focused on its traditional products, like Windows and Office, while competitors like Apple and Google were innovating in new directions. Nadella could have accepted Microsoft's limitations and focused on maintaining its core business. Instead, he shifted the company's mindset from protecting what it had to exploring what it could become. By fostering a culture of experimentation and learning, Nadella empowered Microsoft's employees to think beyond what was and explore what could be. As a result, Microsoft did not just recover—it evolved, leading the way in cloud computing, artificial intelligence, and digital transformation.

When leaders embrace infinite possibilities, they create a culture that encourages risk-taking and innovation. This mindset does not ignore challenges—it embraces them as opportunities for growth.

Rather than fearing failure, leaders who operate from this perspective understand that failure is simply part of the process of discovering new solutions. This reduces the fear that often stifles innovation and encourages teams to explore new ideas, push boundaries, and learn from their mistakes. The result is not only increased creativity but also a more resilient organization, one that is better equipped to navigate uncertainty and change.

This mindset shift also changes how leaders approach opportunities. Traditional leadership may focus on incremental growth—how to make the company a little better, a little more efficient, or a little more profitable. But when leaders adopt a mindset of infinite possibilities, they start to think in terms of transformation rather than optimization. They are no longer satisfied with small improvements; they begin to look for ways to fundamentally reshape their industries, create new markets, and redefine success.

Indra Nooyi's leadership at PepsiCo is a perfect example of this. When Nooyi took over as CEO, PepsiCo was known primarily for its sugary drinks and salty snacks. Many would have focused on optimizing these core products for profitability. But Nooyi had a different vision—rooted in the belief that PepsiCo could be both profitable and purpose-driven. She saw an opportunity to lead the company into the future by expanding its focus to healthier products and sustainability. This shift in mindset allowed PepsiCo to evolve, introducing new product lines that aligned with the growing consumer demand for healthier choices while still maintaining its core business. Nooyi's belief in infinite possibilities enabled her to transform a legacy company into a future-focused leader in both health and sustainability.

The mindset shift toward infinite possibilities also affects how leaders view their teams. Rather than seeing people as resources to be managed, leaders who embrace this perspective see individuals as untapped reservoirs of potential. They understand that their role is not to control but to empower—to create environments where people are free to experiment, innovate, and grow. This leadership approach fosters loyalty, creativity, and a sense of ownership among team members, as they feel valued not just for what they can do now but for what they can become.

Oprah Winfrey exemplifies this approach in her leadership of both her media empire and her philanthropic endeavors. Oprah has always believed in the boundless potential of individuals, and she has built her career on helping others unlock that potential. Whether through her talk show, where she gave voice to underrepresented stories, or her Oprah Winfrey Network, which focuses on inspirational programming, Oprah has consistently demonstrated her belief that people have the ability to grow beyond their circumstances. Her leadership has empowered millions of viewers to see their own potential and has transformed the way media can be used as a tool for personal and collective growth.

The shift to a mindset of infinite possibilities is not about being unrealistic or ignoring the existing challenges. Rather, it is about recognizing that challenges themselves are invitations for innovation. Leaders who embrace this mindset are not limited by the constraints of today's resources, knowledge, or capabilities. Instead, they see every challenge as an opportunity to learn, grow, and discover new solutions. By fostering this mindset, leaders create organizations that are not just reactive but proactive—always looking ahead and always seeking out the next opportunity for transformation.

In today's increasingly complex and unpredictable world, this mindset shift is essential for modern leadership. Leaders who continue to operate from a place of scarcity—believing that resources are limited, opportunities are rare, and failure is something to be avoided—will find themselves falling behind. But those who embrace the mindset of infinite possibilities will find that they are not only better equipped to navigate challenges but also positioned to create a future that is far more expansive, innovative, and impactful than what we can imagine today.

This mindset shift requires courage, resilience, and a willingness to venture into the unknown. But for those leaders who embrace it, the rewards are profound. By focusing on the boundless potential that exists in every challenge and opportunity, leaders can unlock levels of growth and innovation that far exceed what they thought was possible. And in doing so, they pave the way for their teams, organizations, and industries to follow suit, creating a ripple effect of boundless growth that extends far beyond themselves.

As you have read about the concept of infinite potential in leadership and the stories of leaders who have embraced this mindset, it is time to turn the focus inward. The shift toward a growth-oriented mindset starts with reflection, an honest assessment of where you currently see limits in your own leadership approach. The aim of this practical application section is to guide you through exercises that will help you identify those self-imposed limits and develop strategies to shift toward a mindset of growth and boundless possibility.

Exercise 1. Identifying Your Leadership Limits

Start by asking yourself: Where do I currently see limits in my leadership? This exercise is about taking a closer look at areas in your personal and professional life where you may have unknowingly placed boundaries on your own potential or the potential of your team.

Reflect on the following questions:

- **What challenges do I avoid or hesitate to tackle because they seem too difficult or overwhelming?**

- **Are there areas in my leadership where I focus more on managing the status quo rather than seeking new opportunities for growth?**

- **In what ways do I restrict myself, my team, or my organization based on current resources, skills, or knowledge?**

- **Do I often feel constrained by external factors—time, finances, or capabilities—without exploring creative solutions or alternatives?**

- **Where do I see my own abilities or knowledge as "fixed" rather than viewing them as areas for growth?**

Take a few minutes to jot down your thoughts. This exercise will help you gain clarity about the areas where you may have accepted limitations instead of challenging them.

Exercise 2. Reframing Challenges as Opportunities

Now that you have identified some of the areas where you may see limits, the next step is to reframe those limitations as opportunities for growth. In this exercise, select one of the challenges or limitations you wrote down in the first exercise.

Consider the following:

- **How could I approach this challenge differently if my team and I have limitless potential for innovation and growth?**

- **What creative solutions could I explore if I removed the assumption that resources or capabilities are fixed?**

- **How can I shift from a problem-focused mindset to an opportunity-focused mindset in this specific situation?**

- **Who on my team might offer fresh perspectives or ideas that I have not considered yet?**

- **What new skills or knowledge could I develop to address this challenge more effectively?**

As you work through these questions, try to produce at least one actionable idea or strategy that reframes the limitation into an opportunity for growth. This exercise helps shift your focus from what you cannot do to what is possible if you approach the challenge from a mindset of infinite potential.

Exercise 3. Cultivating a Growth-Oriented Team Culture

Leadership is not just about your personal growth—it is about cultivating an environment where others feel empowered to grow as well. In this exercise, think about how you can foster a culture of growth within your team or organization.

Reflect on the following:

- **How do I currently encourage my team to take risks and explore new ideas?**

- **What systems or structures are in place that support continuous learning and development?**

- **Are there ways in which my leadership style could be limiting the creative potential of my team?**

- **How can I create more space for collaboration, experimentation, and innovation within my team?**

- **What behaviors or mindsets can I model to show my team that I value growth and adaptability?**

Develop one or two concrete actions that you can implement to promote a growth-oriented culture. This might involve introducing new initiatives for professional development, creating more opportunities for brainstorming and collaboration, or simply encouraging open dialogue about challenges and potential solutions.

Exercise 4. Visualizing Your Infinite Potential

Visualization can be a powerful tool in cultivating a mindset of infinite possibilities. For this exercise, imagine your future as a leader without any of the constraints you may currently face. Take a moment to picture what your leadership would look like if there were no limits—no resource shortages, no time constraints, no skill gaps.

Think about the following:

- **What would you accomplish if you truly believed there were no limits to your potential or the potential of your organization?**

- **How would you lead differently if you approached every challenge with confidence in your ability to find a solution?**

- **What bold actions would you take if you knew failure was just part of the journey to success?**

- **How would your team or organization be transformed by your leadership?**

Write down your vision of limitless leadership. This vision will serve as a powerful reminder of the potential that exists within you and your team. By regularly revisiting this vision, you can start to shift your mindset from focusing on obstacles to focusing on possibilities.

Bringing It All Together

These exercises are designed to help you take the first steps in shifting from a mindset of limitation to one of infinite possibility. By identifying where you currently see limits, reframing challenges as opportunities, cultivating a growth-oriented culture, and visualizing your boundless potential, you will begin to see your leadership approach transform.

Leadership is a journey—one that requires continuous learning, adaptation, and growth. By embracing a mindset of infinite possibilities, you are setting yourself on a path of leadership that not only elevates your personal capabilities but also drives your team and organization toward long-term success. The journey of leadership continues, and with the tools and strategies we will explore in the coming chapters, you will be equipped to thrive in the contemporary world, where the only limits are the ones you place on yourself.

Chapter 2
The Power of Intentional Limitation

One of the most profound truths of leadership is often counterintuitive: true growth as a leader does not come from controlling every decision or micromanaging every outcome. Instead, it comes from intentionally limiting your own influence and creating space for others to step into leadership roles. This is the paradox of intentional limitation—where the act of stepping back allows both the leader and those around them to grow in ways that would be impossible in an environment of complete control.

In traditional leadership models, power is often equated with control—the idea that a strong leader is one who commands every situation and directs all aspects of their team's efforts. While this may work in the short term or in crises, it stifles long-term growth and innovation. When a leader holds onto control too tightly, they inadvertently limit the potential of those around them. Team members may become dependent on the leader for every decision or feel unable to contribute their ideas and skills. In this kind of environment, the leader may get things done, but the growth of the team—and the leader themself—is stunted.

The paradox of intentional limitation suggests something different. It is the idea that by consciously stepping back, leaders can actually create more opportunities for growth—both for themselves and for their team. When a leader limits their involvement in certain decisions or allow others to take charge of projects, they make space for innovation, creativity, and the development of new leaders within the organization. It is not about abdicating responsibility but empowering others to reach their fullest potential.

This concept is rooted in the belief that leadership is not just about directing others but about nurturing the growth of those around you. By intentionally limiting your own influence, you provide opportunities for others to demonstrate their capabilities, develop their decision-making skills, and take ownership of their work. Over time, this creates a more engaged, capable, and innovative team—one that can function autonomously and continue to grow without constant direction from the top.

Take the example of Howard Schultz, the former CEO of Starbucks. Schultz built a global coffee empire, but he understood that his leadership success was not about controlling every aspect of the business. He created a culture where Starbucks' partners (employees) were empowered to make decisions at every level of the organization, from how they interacted with customers to how stores were managed. Schultz intentionally limited his control over many aspects of the business, allowing others to take ownership of the Starbucks experience. This did not weaken his leadership; instead, it strengthened the company as a whole, creating an engaged workforce that felt valued and capable of making meaningful contributions.

Similarly, Satya Nadella at Microsoft embraced the idea of intentional limitation. Under his leadership, Microsoft shifted from a culture of competition and hierarchy to one of collaboration and empowerment. Nadella understood that for Microsoft to thrive, he needed to create space for his teams to experiment, innovate, and even fail without fear of judgment. By stepping back and giving teams the autonomy to solve problems and develop new ideas, Nadella enabled Microsoft to regain its innovative edge. His intentional limitation allowed the company to grow in directions that a more controlling leader might have stifled.

The paradox here is clear: by stepping back, leaders create the conditions necessary for greater engagement and more dynamic problem-solving. They give their teams the freedom to learn, to grow, and to lead. This does not mean that the leader disappears or abandons their responsibilities. Instead, it means that they are selective about where their energy and attention are most needed and trust their teams to handle the rest.

Intentional limitation also fosters a deeper sense of ownership among team members. When people are trusted with decision-making power and given room to lead, they are more likely to feel accountable for the outcomes. This sense of ownership drives greater motivation, commitment, and creativity. Team members become invested in the success of the project or the organization because they see their contributions as vital to its overall success. The leader, in turn, benefits from the collective wisdom, talents, and ideas of their team—a resource that no single leader can ever fully replicate on their own.

However, the growth that comes from intentional limitation is not just for the team but also for the leader. When leaders release the need to control every detail, they free themselves to focus on higher-level strategic thinking. They can invest more time in envisioning the future, building relationships, and fostering innovation. In fact, the act of limiting oneself can reveal strengths and opportunities in others that the leader may have overlooked. It helps leaders grow in their ability to trust, delegate, and guide their teams without micromanaging. This broader, more expansive form of leadership leads to personal growth as well as organizational success.

The idea of intentional limitation challenges the traditional image of the leader as the all-knowing, all-powerful figure at the center of everything. Instead, it presents leadership as a shared process, one in which the leader empowers others to take on responsibility and to grow alongside them. In this model, leadership is not a one-person job; it is a collective effort where everyone has the chance to contribute and grow.

To embrace this paradox in your own leadership, start by asking yourself: Where can I step back? What decisions or responsibilities can I delegate to others to allow them to grow? How can I create an environment where others feel empowered to take the lead? By consciously limiting your control in these areas, you will begin to see the growth that comes not from doing more but from doing less.

In today's complex and rapidly changing business environment, the ability to empower others is crucial. Leaders who try to control every aspect of their organizations will find themselves overwhelmed, their teams disengaged, and innovation stifled. However, those who practice intentional limitation will create organizations where growth is constant, where new leaders emerge, and where the potential for success is truly boundless.

Throughout history, some of the most transformative leaders have understood a simple yet powerful truth: true leadership is not about exercising power over others but creating space for people to step into their own power. These leaders recognized that their own influence grew not by controlling every decision but by empowering others to take ownership and lead. Whether in political movements or corporate boardrooms, they practiced intentional restraint, allowing others to rise and contribute in ways that led to greater success, innovation, and collective growth.

One of the most profound examples of leadership through restraint comes from Mahatma Gandhi, whose approach to leadership changed the course of history. Gandhi's fight for India's independence from British rule was not waged through force or authoritarian control. Instead, he practiced satyagraha, a philosophy of nonviolent resistance, which was as much about self-restraint as it was about resisting oppression. Gandhi understood that true power did not come from asserting dominance, but from empowering millions of ordinary people to believe in their own ability to effect change.

Gandhi's strategy of restraint—both in his personal life and in his leadership—empowered an entire nation to rise up through peaceful protest. He led by example, demonstrating that restraint could be a powerful form of leadership. By refusing to resort to violence, even in the face of violent opposition, Gandhi showed his followers that they, too, could resist without hatred or aggression. His restraint did not weaken his influence; it amplified it. It created a movement that was inclusive and participatory, allowing millions of people to take ownership of the struggle for independence.

Gandhi's leadership approach was revolutionary because it was not about one person holding power. It was about spreading power across the entire movement. By empowering others to lead their own communities in nonviolent resistance, Gandhi decentralized the movement, making it resilient, adaptable, and, ultimately, unstoppable. His example shows how restraint—far from being a passive act—can be a powerful tool for inspiring collective action and growth.

In the modern corporate world, few leaders have exemplified the paradox of intentional limitation as successfully as Jeff Bezos, the founder of Amazon. From the outset, Bezos believed that Amazon's long-term success would depend on its ability to innovate continuously. However, he also recognized that no single leader, no matter how visionary, could drive innovation alone. Innovation would need to come from every corner of the organization, and for that to happen, Bezos knew he had to give his teams the autonomy to take risks and make decisions.

One of the most famous examples of this approach at Amazon is the company's use of "two-pizza teams." Bezos created small, autonomous teams—no larger than what could be fed with two pizzas—to work on new products or ideas. These teams were given the freedom to experiment, innovate, and fail without constant oversight from upper management. Bezos intentionally limited his direct control over these teams because he understood that the best ideas often come from those closest to the problems being solved.

By practicing restraint and trusting his teams, Bezos created a culture of innovation that allowed Amazon to grow from a small online bookstore into one of the world's most powerful and diversified companies. This strategy of decentralized decision-making and autonomy led to the creation of groundbreaking services like Amazon Web Services (AWS), which started as a small project and grew into a multi-billion-dollar business. Bezos's restraint—his willingness to step back and let others take the lead—was a key factor in Amazon's ability to disrupt industries and stay ahead of its competitors continually.

While the contexts of Gandhi's political leadership and Bezos's corporate leadership could not be more different, the underlying principle remains the same: by practicing restraint and creating space for others to lead, both men achieved extraordinary outcomes. Gandhi empowered millions of Indians to take up the cause of independence in their own communities, creating a decentralized movement that was incredibly difficult to suppress. Bezos empowered small teams within Amazon to innovate autonomously, creating a corporate culture that could respond nimbly to changing market conditions and seize new opportunities as they arose.

Both leaders understood that their personal influence did not need to extend to every decision or every action. By stepping back, they allowed others to step up. This empowered not only individuals but entire movements and organizations to realize their potential.

Leaders who understand the power of intentional limitation create cultures of growth, innovation, and shared ownership. They inspire those around them to think creatively, take risks, and develop their own leadership capacities. This approach not only strengthens the organization but also helps the leader grow by freeing them from the need to control everything and allowing them to focus on long-term vision and strategy.

One of the most significant yet nuanced responsibilities of leadership is finding the right balance between exerting authority and stepping back to create space for others to grow. Leaders are often expected to make decisions, provide direction, and lead from the front. However, the paradox of leadership is that true growth—both for the leader and the team—often comes not from micromanaging every detail but from intentionally stepping back and allowing others to lead. This balance between asserting authority and empowering others is critical for cultivating leadership potential within teams and ensuring long-term success.

Leaders, by definition, are tasked with setting a clear vision, providing direction, and maintaining alignment with organizational goals. There are times when stepping in and asserting authority is absolutely necessary. This is particularly true in moments of crisis, when critical decisions need to be made quickly and decisively or when a team lacks the experience or information needed to navigate complex situations.

When leaders assert authority, they provide clarity and a sense of security. Teams often look to their leaders for guidance in uncertain situations, and clear, authoritative leadership in these moments can provide stability and direction. Assertiveness is also necessary when it comes to setting expectations, holding people accountable, and ensuring that the organization stays aligned with its strategic objectives.

However, while asserting authority is important, it cannot be the default mode of leadership if a leader's goal is to foster growth and innovation. Constantly leading from the front and controlling every decision can stifle creativity, limit personal ownership, and prevent others from stepping into their potential. This is where the art of stepping back comes into play.

Stepping back, as a leader, is about more than simply delegating tasks. It involves creating a space where others feel empowered to make decisions, take risks, and lead. By intentionally stepping back, leaders foster an environment of trust and autonomy—both of which are essential for cultivating leadership potential in others.

When leaders step back, they signal that they trust their team's abilities to handle important responsibilities. This trust can inspire confidence and creativity in team members, giving them the freedom to explore new solutions, make decisions, and even learn from their mistakes. This process of trial and error is crucial for growth. It allows team members to develop critical problem-solving and decision-making skills, which are essential for future leadership roles.

However, stepping back does not mean leaders disappear or relinquish their influence altogether. It is about knowing when to provide space and when to step in to offer support or guidance. Leaders must remain accessible and engaged but refrain from immediately taking control or solving every problem themselves. This balance allows others to experience leadership, make impactful decisions, and grow, all while knowing that the leader is there to provide support if needed.

The key to balancing authority with stepping back lies in discernment. Leaders must be able to assess when it is appropriate to step in and take control and when it is more productive to step back and let others lead. This requires emotional intelligence, trust in the team, and a willingness to embrace the learning process that comes with allowing others to take charge.

Here are a few strategies to help leaders balance authority with empowering others:

Assess the Situation: Leaders should ask themselves whether the situation requires their direct involvement or whether it presents an opportunity for others to step up. For example, in high-stakes situations or when a critical decision needs to be made, stepping in may be necessary. However, in day-to-day operations or when the stakes are lower, stepping back allows others to gain valuable leadership experience.

Delegate with Purpose: Delegation is not about offloading tasks but about giving people meaningful opportunities to lead. When delegating, leaders should choose tasks or projects that align with the team members' growth areas. This gives individuals a chance to develop their skills while contributing to the organization's success.

Create a Safety Net for Risk-Taking: Encouraging others to lead means they will inevitably make mistakes. Leaders must create an environment where taking risks and learning from failure are not only acceptable but encouraged. When team members know that their leader supports them—even when they stumble—they are more likely to take the initiative and grow in their roles.

Provide Clear Expectations and Feedback: Stepping back does not mean abandoning oversight. Leaders should still set clear expectations for what success looks like and provide timely feedback. Constructive feedback, whether positive or critical, helps individuals understand where they excel and can improve.

Maintain Strategic Involvement: Stepping back does not mean stepping out entirely. Leaders should remain involved in a strategic capacity, checking in regularly to provide support, ask insightful questions, and ensure that the team is aligned with broader goals. This involvement shows that the leader is still engaged without micromanaging the process.

Adapt to Team Maturity: Different teams and individuals require different levels of guidance. A leader's approach should evolve based on the experience and maturity of the team. With seasoned teams, leaders can step back more frequently, allowing for greater autonomy. For less experienced teams, leaders may need to offer more support initially but can gradually step back as the team gains confidence and competence.

When leaders step back, they give their team members the gift of autonomy. Autonomy breeds ownership, and ownership breeds growth. Team members who are trusted with real responsibility will develop a deeper sense of commitment to their work and to the success of the organization. They will also gain valuable leadership experience that prepares them for future roles, ensuring that leadership development happens at all levels of the organization.

Additionally, leaders themselves grow when they learn to step back. By allowing others to take on leadership roles, leaders free themselves to focus on higher-level strategic thinking, long-term planning, and relationship-building. Stepping back can also reveal new strengths and capabilities in the team that the leader may not have recognized before. It helps leaders develop the skill of coaching and mentoring rather than managing every detail—a skill that is critical for long-term leadership success.

Ultimately, the balance between asserting authority and stepping back is about trust—trust in the leader's own judgment and trust in the team's potential. By striking this balance, leaders cultivate an environment where leadership is shared, where individuals are empowered to grow, and where the organization becomes stronger, more innovative, and more resilient.

In the modern leadership landscape, this balance is more important than ever. Organizations today require leaders who can be both decisive and empowering—leaders who know when to take charge and when to step back and let others lead. When this balance is achieved, the result is not only a stronger leader but also a stronger, more dynamic team ready to meet the challenges of today and tomorrow.

Intentional limitation is the practice of consciously stepping back as a leader to create space for others to grow, take initiative, and lead.

It is about deliberately refraining from exerting control over every aspect of a team's work and empowering individuals to think for themselves, make decisions, and develop their leadership potential. While this concept might seem counterintuitive to leaders who are used to being the primary decision-makers, it is a powerful technique for cultivating a culture of trust, collaboration, and innovation. Here are several practical tools and exercises that can help leaders apply intentional limitation in their leadership style.

Tool 1. The Delegation Matrix

Effective delegation is one of the most important techniques for applying intentional limitations. The *Delegation Matrix* is a tool that helps leaders evaluate the tasks they should delegate based on two key factors: the importance of the task and the level of expertise required. By using this tool, leaders can determine which tasks can be handed off to others and which tasks require their direct involvement.

How to Use the Delegation Matrix:

1. **List all tasks**: Write down all the key responsibilities and tasks you handle as a leader.

2. **Evaluate importance**: Assign each task a score based on its importance to the overall success of the organization (e.g., 1 = low importance, 5 = critical).

3. **Evaluate expertise**: Assign a score based on how much expertise or experience is required to successfully complete the task (e.g., 1 = minimal expertise, 5 = highly specialized knowledge).

4. **Assign tasks to quadrants**: Place each task into one of the following four quadrants:

    o   **Quadrant 1: Low importance, low expertise**: Delegate immediately. These tasks are neither highly important nor require specific expertise.

    o   **Quadrant 2: High importance, low expertise**: Delegate to someone capable of handling the task with oversight from you. These are tasks where others can step up, but they need some guidance.

    o   **Quadrant 3: Low importance, high expertise**: Consider delegating to those who could benefit from developing expertise in this area. These tasks can help others grow their skills.

- o **Quadrant 4: High importance, high expertise**: Handle these tasks yourself, but look for opportunities to coach others to take them on eventually.

By thoughtfully delegating tasks based on the matrix, leaders allow others to take ownership while ensuring that they are involved in areas where their leadership is most needed.

Tool 2. Empowerment Agreements

Empowerment agreements are a tool leaders can use to provide structure around delegation and intentional limitation. These agreements outline the scope of responsibility, the level of decision-making authority, and the boundaries within which team members can operate independently. They ensure that expectations are clear while also giving individuals the freedom to lead in their assigned areas.

How to Create Empowerment Agreements:

1. **Define the responsibility**: Identify the specific project or task that the team member will take ownership of.

2. **Clarify decision-making authority**: Determine the level of authority the individual has in making decisions without your direct involvement. This could range from making all decisions independently to seeking input only on major issues.

3. **Set boundaries**: Outline any parameters that the individual needs to operate within (e.g., budget limits, timelines, or key milestones).

4. **Agree on check-ins**: Establish a regular check-in schedule to review progress, offer guidance, and provide feedback. The key is to offer support without taking back control of the task.

5. **Review and reflect**: After completing the project or task, review the outcomes together. Discuss what worked, what did not, and how the experience can inform future delegation.

This structured approach allows leaders to step back in a way that feels comfortable for both the leader and the team member, creating a clear path for individual growth.

Exercise 1. Identifying Control Triggers

A critical part of applying intentional limitation is recognizing when, why, and how you tend to assert control. This self-awareness can help you develop the discipline to step back when appropriate. The *Control Trigger Exercise* helps leaders identify situations where they may instinctively take over and how to reframe their responses.

How to Conduct the Control Trigger Exercise:

1. **Reflect on recent decisions**: Think about a few recent situations where you stepped in to take control of a task or decision. What was your reasoning for doing so? Did you feel that it was necessary, or was it an instinctual response?

2. **Identify triggers**: Look for patterns in these situations. Did you step in because the task seemed high-risk? Did you feel uncomfortable with the team's approach? Were you afraid of failure?

3. **Reframe your triggers**: For each trigger you identified, ask yourself, "What could I have done differently to allow others to take the lead?" For example, if the task seemed high-risk, could you have provided guidance without taking control? If the team's approach were different from yours, could you have trusted their methods and allowed them to experiment?

4. **Commit to change**: Write down one or two key areas where you recognize that you need to step back more often. Make a conscious effort to be mindful of these triggers in future situations and remind yourself to apply intentional limitations.

By identifying your control triggers, you can begin to practice restraint in moments when your instinct may be to step in, allowing your team to take greater ownership of their work.

Exercise 2. The Leadership Limitation Journal

The *Leadership Limitation Journal* is a powerful tool for tracking your progress in stepping back and creating space for others to lead. By journaling your experiences, you will be able to reflect on the impact of intentional limitation and identify areas for further improvement.

How to Use the Leadership Limitation Journal:

1. **Set an intention**: At the beginning of each week, write down one or two specific ways you plan to step back and allow others to take more ownership. This could involve delegating a specific task, empowering someone to make a decision, or holding back from intervening in a project.

2. **Track your experiences**: Throughout the week, record moments when you successfully applied intentional limitation. Describe the situation, what you did (or did not do), and the results. Were there moments when you wanted to step in but chose not to? What was the outcome?

3. **Reflect on growth**: At the end of each week, review your entries and reflect on what you learned. How did stepping back impact your team's performance or morale? Did you notice growth in others? Did you learn something new about your own leadership?

4. **Adjust your approach**: Based on your reflections, adjust your approach for the following week. If you felt that you stepped in too often, commit to creating more space for others. If you feel that you have delegated effectively, consider expanding the level of autonomy you give in future situations.

By keeping a journal, you can actively track your progress in applying intentional limitations, ensuring that you remain mindful of when to step back and how to refine your leadership approach.

Tool 3. The Autonomy-Development Ladder

The *Autonomy-Development Ladder* is a technique for gradually increasing the level of autonomy you provide to your team members as they gain experience and confidence. This tool is particularly useful for leaders who want to foster leadership skills in their team but are hesitant to immediately give full control over others.

How to Use the Autonomy-Development Ladder:

1. **Start with guidance**: For newer team members or individuals who are taking on new responsibilities, begin with high involvement. Provide clear instructions, close supervision, and regular feedback.

2. **Increase autonomy gradually**: As the individual demonstrates competence, give them more autonomy. Allow them to make decisions within certain boundaries while still offering guidance when needed.

3. **Move to advisory**: Once the individual has demonstrated confidence in their role, shift your involvement to more of an advisory capacity. Let them come to you with questions, but encourage them to solve problems independently.

4. **Full autonomy**: The final stage is full autonomy, where the individual takes full ownership of the task or project. At this stage, your role is to check in periodically and offer feedback, but the decision-making and execution are entirely in their hands.

Using the Autonomy-Development Ladder, you can gradually build trust and confidence in your team, allowing them to grow into leadership roles while ensuring they are supported along the way.

Intentional limitation is a powerful leadership tool that, when applied thoughtfully, creates a culture where people feel empowered to take ownership, innovate, and lead. By using practical tools like the Delegation Matrix, Empowerment Agreements, and the Autonomy-Development Ladder, and by engaging in reflective exercises like the Control Trigger Exercise and Leadership Limitation Journal, leaders can strike the right balance between guiding their teams and giving them the space to grow.

Stepping back does not mean stepping away—it means creating the conditions for others to step up, building a stronger, more capable team, and ultimately becoming a more effective leader.

Chapter 3
The Ten Dimensions of Leadership Mastery

At the heart of *Infinite Potential Leadership* lie ten interconnected dimensions that, together, form the foundation of truly transformative leadership. These dimensions represent the essential qualities that every leader must cultivate to unlock their own potential and the potential of those they lead. While each dimension can stand on its own, it is their interplay that creates a dynamic, holistic model of leadership, one that equips leaders to navigate complexity, foster innovation, and drive long-lasting change.

The ten dimensions of leadership mastery—**Vision, Wisdom, Understanding, Compassion, Discipline, Harmony, Resilience, Humility, Integrity, and Stewardship**—are not simply a set of traits to be checked off or mastered in isolation. They work together, influencing and reinforcing each other. Together, they guide leaders to move beyond conventional approaches, empowering them to lead with clarity, empathy, and adaptability in today's rapidly changing world.

Vision is where leadership begins. It is the ability to see beyond the present and imagine a compelling future that inspires others. Leaders with vision do not just focus on the immediate challenges or opportunities; they set a direction that others can rally behind. Vision is forward-thinking and aspirational, acting as a beacon that unites teams and drives collective effort. It provides purpose and clarity, ensuring that everyone understands not just what they are doing but why they are doing it. Without vision, leadership lacks focus and momentum. It is the dimension that ignites all others, fueling the passion and purpose necessary for growth and innovation.

Vision is more than just setting goals—it is the ability to clearly see the future and inspire others to move toward it. A compelling vision provides a sense of direction, but a truly transformative vision also aligns with the deeper purpose and values of an organization. The most effective leaders do not just articulate what needs to be done; they communicate a powerful narrative about why it matters. This sense of shared purpose motivates individuals and aligns efforts across the organization, ensuring that every action contributes to a larger goal.

To deepen vision, leaders must continually refine their ability to anticipate trends, assess risks, and identify opportunities that others might overlook. This means staying curious, challenging assumptions, and remaining open to new possibilities. Visionary leaders are adept at looking beyond the current landscape, drawing from diverse perspectives, and understanding the broader social, economic, and technological forces shaping the future. They are willing to take calculated risks in pursuit of their vision, knowing that bold ideas often lead to transformative change.

A deep vision also requires self-awareness. Leaders must align their personal values with their organizational goals to ensure authenticity. When the leader's vision reflects their own passion and commitment, it resonates more deeply with others, fostering greater loyalty and dedication from their teams.

While vision shows the way forward, wisdom ensures that the path is navigated thoughtfully. **Wisdom** is the dimension that blends knowledge, experience, and intuition. It allows leaders to make sound decisions in the face of uncertainty, to balance competing priorities, and to see the bigger picture. Wisdom goes beyond data and analytics; it is about knowing when to trust the numbers and when to rely on deeper insights. Wise leaders are not only strategic but also reflective, taking into account both short-term outcomes and long-term impact. Wisdom tempers vision, ensuring that leaders move forward with purpose, care, and consideration.

Wisdom is the art of making decisions that are both informed and insightful. It combines the rational use of data and logic with the leader's capacity for intuitive understanding—a skill that often comes from years of experience and a deep awareness of human dynamics. Wise leaders understand that while data is essential for making informed choices, it must be complemented by the ability to read situations that cannot be fully quantified.

Going deeper, wisdom requires reflection. Leaders who practice wisdom do not just react to circumstances; they take time to analyze, interpret, and anticipate the long-term implications of their actions. They look beyond the immediate facts to consider the ripple effects of their decisions on people, processes, and future opportunities. This requires a balance of patience and decisiveness—knowing when to wait for more information and when to act with conviction.

Wisdom also encompasses the ability to navigate ambiguity. In the fast-paced, unpredictable landscape of modern business, wise leaders are comfortable making decisions even when all the answers are not clear. They use their experience to fill in the gaps and trust their judgment when faced with uncertainty. This nuanced approach to decision-making helps organizations remain agile and adaptable in the face of change.

Furthermore, wisdom involves an ethical dimension. Wise leaders not only make decisions that benefit the organization but also consider the broader impact on stakeholders, communities, and the environment. Their choices reflect a commitment to doing what is right, not just what is profitable.

Understanding is the dimension that connects leaders to the people they lead. It is about empathy, active listening, and the ability to see the world through the eyes of others. Leaders with understanding build trust, strengthen relationships, and create environments where people feel valued and heard. This dimension is critical in today's diverse and rapidly changing organizations. Without understanding, even the most visionary leader can become disconnected from their team, failing to address the real concerns and motivations that drive performance. Understanding complements wisdom by ensuring that decisions are informed by the perspectives and needs of others, creating a more inclusive and effective leadership approach.

Understanding goes beyond intellectual comprehension; it involves emotional and relational intelligence. Leaders with deep understanding do not just analyze data or listen to feedback; they seek to truly grasp the needs, concerns, and motivations of their people. This dimension is essential for fostering trust, loyalty, and collaboration in any organization.

Leaders who excel in understanding, practice empathic listening – which means engaging with others without judgment and seeking to fully comprehend their perspectives before offering responses. Empathic listening helps leaders build stronger relationships with their teams by showing that they value input and are open to different viewpoints. It is through understanding that leaders can unlock the full potential of their teams, as individuals feel heard, respected, and motivated to contribute their best efforts.

Understanding requires the ability to navigate cultural, generational, and experiential differences within a team. In today's increasingly diverse work environments, leaders must be adept at bridging these gaps and integrating a variety of perspectives into the decision-making process. Understanding diverse viewpoints does not just create a more inclusive environment—it leads to better problem-solving and innovation.

Leaders who develop deep understanding also become more effective communicators. They tailor their communication styles to resonate with different audiences, ensuring that their messages are clear and impactful across various contexts. This ability to connect with others on both an intellectual and emotional level strengthens a leader's influence and effectiveness.

Closely related to understanding, **Compassion** is the emotional intelligence that leaders use to care for the well-being of their teams. Compassionate leaders foster cultures of kindness where people feel supported in both their professional and personal lives. This dimension goes beyond understanding individual perspectives—it involves actively helping others grow, heal, and thrive. Compassion creates loyalty and engagement, as people are naturally drawn to leaders who genuinely care for them. When combined with understanding, compassion deepens relationships and enhances collaboration, creating an environment where individuals are not only motivated but also inspired to contribute their best.

Compassion in leadership is more than kindness—it is the genuine concern for the well-being and growth of others. Compassionate leaders understand that fostering a healthy, supportive work environment leads to higher levels of engagement, productivity, and innovation. They go beyond surface-level interactions and take the time to understand the unique challenges and aspirations of their team members.

To lead with compassion, leaders must develop emotional intelligence. This means not only being aware of their own emotions but also recognizing and responding to the emotions of others. Compassionate leaders are skilled at providing the right balance of support and challenge—pushing their teams to grow while offering the empathy and resources needed to overcome obstacles.

At its deepest level, compassion fosters loyalty and commitment. When team members feel that their leaders truly care about their success and well-being, they are more likely to go above and beyond in their efforts. Compassion also plays a critical role in conflict resolution. Leaders who practice compassion can address tensions and disagreements in ways that heal and strengthen relationships, rather than allowing conflicts to fester.

Furthermore, compassionate leaders understand the broader impact of their actions on the community and society. They consider how their decisions affect not only the bottom line but also the lives of the people within and beyond the organization. Compassionate leadership, therefore, is not just about nurturing individuals—it is about contributing to the greater good.

While compassion nurtures the emotional side of leadership, **Discipline** ensures accountability and focus. Discipline is the dimension that drives consistency, hard work, and the ability to maintain course even when the journey gets difficult. Leaders with discipline set high standards for themselves and their teams, ensuring that vision is not just a lofty goal but something that is systematically worked toward. Discipline keeps the team on track, ensuring that actions align with intentions. Without discipline, even the most visionary plans can falter. It is the structure that ensures sustainable progress and long-term success.

Discipline is the structure that translates vision into action. While vision and creativity inspire teams, discipline ensures that these ideas are executed precisely and consistently. Leaders with strong discipline create systems, processes, and habits that drive performance and accountability. They know how to set clear expectations, track progress, and make adjustments as needed to keep the team aligned with its goals.

At its core, discipline is about focus. In a world full of distractions and competing priorities, disciplined leaders know how to maintain their attention on what truly matters. They are skilled at setting boundaries and saying no to initiatives that do not align with the organization's core objectives. This ability to prioritize ensures that resources—whether time, talent, or capital—are used effectively.

However, discipline is not about rigidity. Effective leaders balance discipline with flexibility, recognizing that circumstances can change and plans may need to be adjusted. The key is maintaining a clear focus on the end goal while being adaptable in the methods used to achieve it. Leaders who cultivate discipline create a culture of accountability where everyone understands their role in moving the organization forward.

Discipline also requires self-mastery. Leaders must hold themselves to high standards, modeling the behavior they expect from others. This includes managing their time effectively, maintaining emotional composure, and consistently delivering on their commitments. Through disciplined leadership, teams develop the resilience and focus needed to overcome challenges and achieve long-term success.

Harmony is the ability to balance competing priorities and integrate diverse perspectives. It is about creating unity in complexity. In any leadership role, conflicts will arise—between short-term and long-term goals, between individual needs and organizational objectives, or between different ways of approaching a problem. Leaders who cultivate harmony are able to navigate these conflicts in a way that brings people together rather than pulling them apart. Harmony fosters collaboration and alignment, ensuring everyone works toward the same overarching vision. It also connects with compassion and understanding, as it requires the leader to consider multiple viewpoints and create synergy among them.

Harmony is the ability to integrate diverse perspectives and balance competing priorities in a way that fosters collaboration and alignment. In any organization, tensions will always exist between short-term and long-term goals, individual and collective needs, and different ways of approaching problems. Leaders who cultivate harmony excel at navigating these tensions and finding solutions that bring people together rather than pulling them apart.

At its essence, harmony is about inclusivity. Leaders who foster harmony ensure that all voices are heard and considered in decision-making. This does not mean avoiding conflict or trying to please everyone. Instead, it involves creating a space where differing opinions can be openly discussed and compromises can be reached that serve the greater good. By integrating diverse viewpoints, leaders build more robust strategies and solutions.

Furthermore, harmony is critical for managing organizational change. During times of transformation, leaders must align their teams around a shared vision while acknowledging the uncertainties and challenges that come with change. Leaders who practice harmony guide their teams through these transitions with empathy, ensuring that everyone feels supported and engaged in the process.

Harmony also plays a vital role in maintaining balance within the leaders themselves. Effective leadership requires balancing ambition with self-care and drive with reflection. Leaders who are in harmony with themselves are better equipped to maintain their energy, manage stress, and sustain their leadership over the long term.

Resilience is the dimension that keeps leaders and their teams moving forward in the face of setbacks. In today's world, change is constant, and challenges are inevitable. Resilient leaders know how to recover from failure, adapt to new circumstances, and maintain a positive outlook even when things do not go as planned. Resilience is about staying the course, learning from mistakes, and maintaining the energy to push through adversity. It strengthens discipline by ensuring that even when the road gets tough, leaders and their teams have the emotional and mental endurance to keep going.

Resilience is the dimension that enables leaders to persevere in the face of adversity, uncertainty, and setbacks. It is the ability to remain steadfast and optimistic, even when challenges seem insurmountable. In today's fast-paced and unpredictable world, resilience is a critical trait for leaders who must navigate constant change, disruption, and unforeseen obstacles.

At its core, resilience is about adaptability and grit. Leaders who cultivate resilience are not only able to recover from failures but also to use those experiences as opportunities for learning and growth. They understand that setbacks are part of the journey toward success and develop the mental fortitude to continue pushing forward, even when the path is difficult.

Resilience is also closely tied to emotional intelligence. Leaders who are resilient are able to regulate their emotions, maintaining calm and composure during stressful situations. This emotional stability enables them to make rational decisions and guide their teams through turbulence without succumbing to panic or despair. By modeling resilience, leaders create a culture where challenges are seen as opportunities for growth rather than reasons for fear.

Moreover, resilience is not just about individual toughness—it is about fostering a resilient culture within the organization. Leaders must create environments where teams feel supported in taking risks, experimenting, and learning from their mistakes. This culture of resilience encourages innovation and prevents the fear of failure from stifling creativity. When individuals know that they can recover from setbacks, they are more likely to push boundaries and pursue bold ideas.

To build resilience, leaders must focus on both their physical and mental well-being. This involves managing stress, practicing self-care, and developing coping strategies that allow them to bounce back from difficult situations. Leaders who prioritize resilience not only improve their own ability to lead but also inspire their teams to stay motivated and optimistic, even in the face of uncertainty.

Humility is what grounds leadership in reality. Leaders with humility recognize that they do not have all the answers and are willing to learn from others, admit mistakes, and seek guidance when needed. Humility fosters a growth mindset, where leaders are always looking for ways to improve themselves and their organizations. It also connects deeply with understanding and compassion, as humble leaders are more likely to listen to others and give credit where it is due. Humility allows leaders to be open to new ideas and perspectives, which is essential for innovation and growth.

Humility is the quality that keeps leaders grounded, even in positions of power and influence. It is the recognition that no one has all the answers and that leadership is a shared process. Humble leaders are open to feedback, willing to admit their mistakes, and constantly seek to learn and grow. They understand that their success is often the result of collective efforts and that their role is to serve the organization, not to dominate it.

At its deepest level, humility is about understanding one's own limitations and being comfortable with vulnerability. Leaders who embrace humility are not afraid to say, "I don't know," or to ask for help when needed. This openness fosters a culture of collaboration, where team members feel empowered to contribute their own expertise and perspectives. Humble leaders build trust by showing that they value the input and contributions of others, and they encourage a culture of continuous improvement.

Humility also plays a key role in developing emotional intelligence. Leaders who are humble are more attuned to the needs and feelings of those around them. They are better listeners, more empathetic, and more willing to put the interests of their team ahead of their own ego. This creates an environment of psychological safety, where individuals feel free to express their ideas, ask questions, and challenge assumptions without fear of judgment.

However, humility does not mean being passive or lacking confidence. Humble leaders are still decisive and assertive when necessary, but they approach leadership with a sense of curiosity and openness. They are confident in their abilities but do not let that confidence blind them to the value of others' insights. This balance between confidence and humility is what makes leaders more approachable and effective, as they are seen as both strong and relatable.

To cultivate humility, leaders must practice self-reflection, actively seek feedback, and remain open to learning from their experiences. This involves regularly assessing their own performance and being willing to make changes when necessary. Leaders who embody humility create an environment where everyone is encouraged to grow, innovate, and contribute to the collective success of the organization.

Integrity is the foundation of trust in leadership. It is the alignment of actions with values. Leaders with integrity are consistent, honest, and ethical in their decision-making. This dimension ensures that leaders act in ways that are aligned with their vision and values, even when faced with difficult choices. Integrity is the glue that holds the other dimensions together. Without it, leadership loses credibility, and the trust necessary for effective leadership is eroded. Integrity also strengthens wisdom and discipline, as it demands that leaders stay true to their principles even when it is challenging to do so.

Integrity is the cornerstone of leadership. It is the dimension that ensures a leader's actions are consistently aligned with their values and principles. Leaders with integrity act with honesty, transparency, and ethical commitment, even when faced with difficult choices or pressure to compromise. This consistency in word and action builds trust, both within the organization and with external stakeholders.

At its essence, integrity is about doing the right thing, even when it is not the easiest or most convenient option. Leaders with integrity prioritize long-term ethical considerations over short-term gains, ensuring that their decisions contribute to the overall good of the organization, its people, and the wider community. This ethical foundation is what allows leaders to build lasting credibility and foster deep loyalty among their teams.

Integrity is not just about avoiding wrongdoing but actively promoting a culture of accountability and transparency. Leaders who practice integrity hold themselves and others to high ethical standards. They create clear expectations around behavior and decision-making, ensuring that everyone in the organization understands the importance of acting with honesty and respect. This culture of integrity not only builds trust but also enhances the organization's reputation, attracting employees, partners, and customers who share similar values.

Integrity is closely linked to authenticity. Leaders with integrity are genuine in their interactions, showing up as their true selves rather than trying to project a false image. This authenticity fosters deeper connections with their teams, as people are more likely to trust and follow leaders who are consistent in their values and actions. Authentic leaders inspire others to act with integrity as well, creating a ripple effect that strengthens the moral fabric of the entire organization.

To cultivate integrity, leaders must consistently evaluate their own actions and decisions, ensuring they align with their core values. This involves being transparent about their decision-making processes, admitting mistakes when they occur, and holding themselves accountable to the same standards they expect from others. Integrity is the dimension that grounds all other aspects of leadership, ensuring that success is achieved not only through skill and strategy but also through ethical leadership.

Stewardship is the recognition that leadership is not about personal gain but about serving others and taking responsibility for the growth of the organization and its people. It is about leading with a long-term view, ensuring that the actions taken today contribute to the sustainability and well-being of future generations. Leaders who practice stewardship understand that their role is to guide, nurture, and protect the organization, its values, and its people. Stewardship brings together all the dimensions—vision, wisdom, understanding, and more—into a leadership model that is deeply responsible and future-oriented.

Stewardship is the dimension of leadership that reflects a deep sense of responsibility toward the people, resources, and mission entrusted to a leader's care. Leaders who practice stewardship understand that their role is not just about achieving personal success or short-term gains but about ensuring the long-term health and growth of the organization and its people. Stewardship is about leaving a lasting legacy that benefits future generations, rather than focusing solely on immediate outcomes.

At its core, stewardship is about service. Leaders with a stewardship mindset view themselves as caretakers of the organization's mission, culture, and resources. They prioritize the well-being and development of their teams, creating opportunities for individuals to grow both personally and professionally. Stewardship involves making decisions that ensure the sustainability of the organization, from financial stability to environmental responsibility, and it requires leaders to think long-term.

Stewardship also reflects a commitment to developing future leaders. Leaders who embrace stewardship are intentional about mentoring, coaching, and empowering others to take on leadership roles within the organization. They understand that their legacy will be measured not only by what they achieve during their tenure but also by the strength and capability of the leaders they leave behind. By investing in the growth of others, steward leaders ensure that their organization continues to thrive long after they have moved on.

Stewardship extends beyond the organization itself. It involves a broader commitment to the community and the environment. Leaders with a stewardship mindset consider how their decisions impact not only their employees and customers but also society at large. This could include adopting sustainable business practices, supporting community initiatives, or advocating for social justice. Stewardship-oriented leaders recognize that their influence carries a responsibility to contribute to the greater good.

To cultivate stewardship, leaders must focus on the long-term impact of their decisions and actions. This requires a shift from a mindset of control to one of service, where the leader's primary goal is to support and nurture the growth of others and the sustainability of the organization. Steward leaders create a lasting legacy by ensuring that their organization and its people are well-positioned for future success, contributing to a better world through their leadership.

These ten dimensions are not isolated traits but deeply interconnected and mutually reinforcing. Vision sets the direction, but wisdom ensures that the path forward is thoughtful. Understanding and compassion build strong relationships, while discipline and resilience keep the team focused and motivated. Harmony integrates differing perspectives, humility keeps the leader grounded, integrity builds trust, and stewardship ensures that the leader's legacy is one of service and sustainability.

Together, these dimensions create a holistic leadership model that enables leaders to navigate the complexities of modern organizations while unlocking the infinite potential within themselves and those they lead.

To bring the ten dimensions of leadership into practice, it is important to take time for self-reflection and structured exercises to help you build each dimension of your leadership style. The following are specific tools and exercises that correspond to each leadership dimension, guiding you through intentional practice and growth in each area.

By using these tools and exercises, leaders can deepen their integration of the leadership dimensions into their daily practice. Through reflection, action, and continual adjustment, you will begin to see these dimensions not just as abstract qualities but as living parts of your leadership style that drive transformation in yourself, your team, and your organization.

Vision: Creating a Clear, Compelling Future Direction

Tool 1. Vision Clarity Canvas

The Vision Clarity Canvas helps leaders refine and communicate their vision in a way that is actionable and inspiring.

How to Use the Vision Clarity Canvas:

1. **Define Your Long-Term Goal:** Write down where you see the organization or team in 5 to 10 years. Be specific and vivid in describing the future state.

2. **Break it Down:** Identify 3-5 key milestones that will help your team reach this long-term goal. What steps will you take in the short, medium, and long term to move toward your vision?

3. **Connect with Values:** Ask yourself: How does this vision align with my personal values and the core values of the organization? Ensure the vision resonates on both a practical and emotional level.

4. **Communicate the Vision:** Draft a compelling statement summarising the vision that excites and motivates your team. Share this vision regularly, making it a touchstone for decisions and actions.

Reflection Exercise:

- Review your vision statement every six months and adjust it based on new insights or changes in the external environment.

- Ask yourself: "How well does this vision inspire action? Do I see alignment between daily tasks and the long-term goal?"

Wisdom: Making Decisions that Blend Logic with Intuition

Tool 2. Decision Matrix

The Decision Matrix helps leaders make thoughtful choices by considering both analytical data and intuition.

How to Use the Decision Matrix:

1. **List Key Decisions:** Identify a few important decisions you are facing. Write them down in the matrix.

2. **Evaluate the Data:** For each decision, rate how much data is available to inform the choice (on a scale of 1-10).

3. **Assess Your Intuition:** Reflect on your gut feeling or instinct about each decision. Rate your confidence in these instincts (on a scale of 1-10).

4. **Weigh Both Sides:** For each decision, assess the balance between relying on data versus intuition. Are you favoring one too heavily? What adjustments can you make to strike the right balance?

5. **Take Action:** Based on this assessment, make the decision while integrating both logical analysis and intuitive insights.

Reflection Exercise:

- After each major decision, review the outcome and ask, "How well did I balance data with intuition? What can I learn from this for future decisions?"

Understanding: Analytical Thinking and Deep Listening

Tool 3. Active Listening Journal

The Active Listening Journal is designed to help leaders become more intentional about truly understanding others.

How to Use the Active Listening Journal:

1. **Choose Conversations:** Over the next week, select 3-5 key conversations where you want to practice active listening. This could be one-on-one meetings, team discussions, or even casual check-ins.

2. **Practice Deep Listening:** During these conversations, focus fully on the speaker. Avoid interrupting or thinking about your response while they are speaking. Reflect on their words and emotions.

3. **Journal Your Observations:** After each conversation, write down what you heard. Note not only the words but also the underlying emotions or concerns expressed.

4. **Reflect on Your Listening:** How well did you understand the other person's point of view? Did you notice any biases or distractions that affected your ability to listen fully?

5. **Apply Insights:** Use your observations to inform your leadership approach. For example, how might you adjust your communication style to better align with your team's needs?

Reflection Exercise:

- Once a month, review your journal entries and assess patterns. Are there common themes or concerns your team is raising? How can you better address these in your leadership?

Compassion: Leading with Empathy and Humanity

Tool 4. Empathy Map

The Empathy Map helps leaders understand the emotional needs of their team members and foster a more compassionate environment.

How to Use the Empathy Map:

1. **Identify a Team Member:** Choose a specific team member or group you want to understand better.

2. **Map the Experience:** Divide a sheet into four quadrants: **What they think, What they feel, What they say,** and **What they do.** Reflect on these questions for the team members. What might they be thinking or feeling that they are not saying? How do their words and actions align or differ from their emotions?

3. **Reflect on Their Challenges:** Consider the personal or professional challenges they may be facing. What support might they need from you?

4. **Take Compassionate Action:** Based on your insights, take a specific action to demonstrate empathy and support. This could be offering help, scheduling a one-on-one meeting to listen, or providing flexibility if they are dealing with stress.

Reflection Exercise:

- Reflect weekly on how your compassionate actions are impacting your relationship with your team. Ask yourself: "Am I balancing compassion with accountability? How are my actions fostering trust and well-being?"

Discipline: Setting Boundaries and Maintaining Accountability

Tool 5. Accountability Tracker

The Accountability Tracker is a tool to help leaders maintain both personal and team discipline by setting clear goals and tracking progress.

How to Use the Accountability Tracker:

1. **Set Specific Goals:** Write down 3-5 specific goals for the upcoming month. These should be aligned with your broader vision.

2. **Define Metrics:** For each goal, define how you will measure success. What does progress look like?

3. **Create a Routine:** Establish a routine for tracking your progress (e.g., weekly progress reviews toward these goals).

4. **Hold Yourself Accountable:** Share these goals with a trusted colleague or coach to help keep you accountable. For team goals, clearly communicate these goals and expectations to your team.

5. **Track Progress:** Update your tracker regularly, marking achievements and noting areas where you might be falling behind. Use this as a guide for adjusting efforts and reinforcing discipline.

Reflection Exercise:

- At the end of the month, review your tracker. Ask: "How well did I follow through on my commitments? Where did discipline pay off, and where must I improve my focus?"

Harmony: Balancing Conflicting Priorities and Integrating Diverse Perspectives

Tool 6. Priority Map

The Priority Map is a tool designed to help leaders balance multiple priorities while maintaining organizational harmony.

How to Use the Priority Map:

1. **List Competing Priorities:** Write down all the major priorities or goals you are currently managing. Include both short-term and long-term initiatives.

2. **Assess Importance and Urgency:** Assign each priority a rating based on urgency and importance. Use the Eisenhower Matrix (Important/Urgent, Important/Not Urgent, Not Important/Urgent, Not Important/Not Urgent) to categorize your priorities.

3. **Identify Conflicts:** Highlight areas where priorities conflict, either in terms of resources or attention. Are there trade-offs that need to be made?

4. **Collaborate for Alignment:** Engage with your team to discuss how to balance these priorities. Encourage open dialogue to address conflicting goals and seek ways to harmonize efforts.

Reflection Exercise:

- Once a quarter, review your priority map and ask: "Are we striking the right balance between competing goals? How can I create more alignment and synergy across different initiatives?"

Resilience: Navigating Adversity and Uncertainty with Grit

Tool 7. Resilience Action Plan

The Resilience Action Plan is a tool designed to help leaders build and maintain resilience by identifying challenges, developing coping strategies, and creating a support network.

How to Use the Resilience Action Plan:

1. **Identify Current Challenges:** List the major challenges or stressors you currently face, both personally and professionally. This helps bring clarity to the pressures you are dealing with.

2. **Assess Impact:** For each challenge, assess its potential impact on your leadership effectiveness, emotional well-being, and overall performance.

3. **Develop Coping Strategies:** Write down specific strategies for managing each challenge. This could include stress-reduction techniques, reframing negative situations, or delegating tasks to ease your workload.

4. **Build Your Support Network:** Identify key people—colleagues, mentors, friends, or family—whom you can lean on for support when faced with adversity. Reflect on how often you seek their guidance and whether you should increase those interactions.

5. **Track Your Resilience:** Regularly monitor your emotional and mental state. Are your strategies working? Where can you improve?

Reflection Exercise:

- Every two weeks, revisit your Resilience Action Plan and ask: "What am I learning about myself in times of challenge? How can I better manage my stress and setbacks moving forward?"

Humility: Leading with a Grounded Sense of Self and Appreciation for Others

Tool 8. Humility Check-In

The Humility Check-In is designed to help leaders regularly assess their ability to lead with humility, acknowledge others' contributions, and foster a collaborative spirit.

How to Use the Humility Check-In:

1. **Assess Self-Reflection:** Begin each week by asking yourself, "Where do I need to grow as a leader?" Identify specific areas where you may need to listen, learn, or step back from control.

2. **Solicit Feedback:** Create a habit of asking your team or peers for feedback. This could be as simple as asking, "What could I be doing better to support you?"

3. **Recognize Contributions:** Make it a practice to acknowledge the achievements and contributions of others. Aim to highlight the strengths of your team members in meetings or one-on-one conversations.

4. **Celebrate Team Wins:** Regularly shift the focus from your own success to the success of the team. When your team achieves a goal, emphasize their efforts rather than taking personal credit.

Reflection Exercise:

- Every month, reflect on your humility check-ins and ask: "How well am I listening to others? Am I giving enough credit to my team for their contributions? How can I better foster a culture of learning and collaboration?"

Integrity: Aligning Values with Actions

Tool 9. Values-to-Actions Checklist

The Values-to-Actions Checklist helps leaders ensure their daily decisions and behaviors are aligned with their core values and the ethical standards of their organization.

How to Use the Values-to-Actions Checklist:

1. **Clarify Your Core Values:** Write down your top five personal and leadership values (e.g., honesty, transparency, fairness, accountability).

2. **Identify Key Decisions:** Over the next month, identify three to five significant decisions you need to make, both personally and professionally.

3. **Align with Values:** For each decision, cross-check your values. Ask: "How does this decision align with my core values? Will it strengthen trust and transparency in my leadership?"

4. **Reflect on Impact:** After making these decisions, assess the outcomes. Did your actions align with your stated values? If not, what adjustments can you make moving forward?

Reflection Exercise:

*   At the end of each quarter, ask yourself: "Am I consistently acting in alignment with my values? Where have I compromised, and how can I correct course?"

Stewardship: Being Responsible for the Growth of Others and the Organization

Tool 10. Stewardship Development Plan

The Stewardship Development Plan helps leaders focus on building a legacy of growth by developing others and ensuring the sustainability of the organization.

How to Use the Stewardship Development Plan:

1. **Identify Potential Leaders:** List team members who show promise and leadership potential. Reflect on how you can support their growth.

2. **Create Growth Opportunities:** For each individual, identify specific opportunities for leadership development. This could include mentorship, stretch assignments, or leadership training programs.

3. **Assess Long-Term Impact:** Think about the long-term impact of your decisions on the organization's sustainability. Are your current actions contributing to the future health of the team or business? What legacy are you building?

4. **Engage in Mentorship:** Actively mentor or coach at least one team member. Focus on helping them develop leadership skills and encourage them to think about the broader mission of the organization.

Reflection Exercise:

- Every six months, reflect on your stewardship efforts and ask: "How am I helping develop future leaders? What more can I do to ensure the long-term growth and sustainability of my organization?"

Chapter 4
The Leader as a Node in an
Interconnected System

Leadership does not exist in isolation. At its core, leadership is part of an interconnected system, a web of relationships, influences, and dynamics that stretch far beyond any one individual. Leaders are not only agents of change within their organizations and teams, but they are also shaped by those very systems in which they operate. This interconnectedness means that leadership is both a deeply personal and profoundly social activity, influenced by the collective energy, culture, and structures around it.

In this context, leaders influence—and are influenced by—their teams, organizations, and broader societal structures. This reciprocal relationship emphasizes that effective leadership is about understanding and managing these multiple levels of connection. A leader's decisions ripple outward, impacting the people they lead, the culture of the organization, and, in some cases, the broader community. At the same time, those same leaders are shaped by the feedback they receive from their teams, the structures of their organizations, and the societal norms that frame what leadership should look like.

One of the most immediate levels where leadership exerts influence is within teams. Leaders are responsible for setting the vision, tone, and culture guiding teams' operations. They influence how team members collaborate, innovate, and approach problem-solving. Through their communication style, decision-making approach, and behavior, leaders directly impact the motivation, engagement, and productivity of their teams.

For instance, a leader who practices transparency and open communication will foster a culture of trust where team members feel empowered to share ideas and take risks. Conversely, a leader who micromanages or withholds information might create an atmosphere of fear or disengagement, stifling creativity and reducing the team's overall performance. The behavior and attitudes of leaders cascade through teams, often setting the standard for what is expected and accepted within the group.

This influence is not a one-way street. Leaders are also shaped by the feedback they receive from their teams. The attitudes, emotions, and performance of team members often reflect on the leader, providing insights into the effectiveness of their leadership style. Leaders who are attuned to this feedback can adjust their strategies, becoming more responsive to the needs and concerns of their teams. This creates a dynamic interplay where leaders and teams co-evolve, learning and growing together in a cycle of continuous improvement.

Beyond individual teams, leaders play a critical role in shaping the broader culture of their organizations. They are the architects of the environment in which their teams work, and their values, priorities, and behaviors are mirrored in the organization's structure, policies, and practices. An organization's culture often reflects its leadership, influencing everything from employee engagement to ethical behavior and innovation.

Leaders who foster a culture of inclusion and collaboration create organizations where diverse voices are heard and innovation thrives. They encourage shared decision-making, distribute leadership across all levels, and prioritize professional development for their employees. In contrast, leaders who prioritize hierarchy and control may cultivate environments where communication flows only in one direction, limiting the potential for creativity and shared ownership of outcomes.

However, just as leaders shape organizational culture, they are also shaped by the existing culture of the organization. When leaders enter a new role or inherit an established organization, they are often met with deeply ingrained norms, practices, and values that influence how they lead. Understanding this pre-existing culture is essential for leaders who want to create meaningful change. A leader's ability to influence culture depends on their sensitivity to these structures and their willingness to work within or challenge them to drive transformation.

Leaders are influenced by the power dynamics, systems, and structures of their organizations. These structures can either support or constrain a leader's efforts. For instance, leaders operating within a rigid hierarchical system may find it more challenging to implement collaborative or innovative practices compared to those working in more flexible, decentralized organizations.

Leadership does not exist in a vacuum—leaders are influenced by societal structures, trends, and expectations. Cultural norms, economic conditions, technological advancements, and political climates all shape the way leaders are perceived and how they must operate. Today's leaders must be more attuned than ever to the larger social context in which they function. Issues such as corporate social responsibility, environmental sustainability, diversity, equity, and inclusion are no longer peripheral concerns but central to how leadership is evaluated and judged.

For example, in the wake of global movements for social justice and environmental sustainability, leaders are increasingly expected to take stands on societal issues that go beyond profit and productivity. Stakeholders, including employees, customers, and the public, are holding leaders accountable for their organization's impact on the world. As such, leaders must navigate the complexities of public opinion, regulatory environments, and the changing expectations of being a responsible and ethical leader in today's world.

At the same time, societal forces also shape leadership styles. The rise of remote work, digital transformation, and the increasing importance of mental health in the workplace are trends that leaders must integrate into their strategies. Leaders who can understand and adapt to these societal changes are better equipped to lead organizations that are not only successful but also resilient in the face of future challenges.

Ultimately, leadership is about understanding the system in which one operates and learning how to influence that system while being influenced by it. Leaders must learn to think systemically, recognizing the interconnectedness of their decisions, behaviors, and the broader organizational and societal context. This requires a combination of self-awareness, strategic thinking, and adaptability.

Leaders who understand this interconnected nature are more likely to make decisions that account for both the immediate and long-term impacts on their teams, organizations, and communities. They recognize that leadership is not a solitary endeavor but a collective process that involves listening, learning, and adjusting based on feedback from all parts of the system. This systems-thinking approach allows leaders to create more sustainable, resilient organizations that are capable of thriving in an increasingly complex and interconnected world.

Leadership is not a linear or isolated role. It is a dynamic, reciprocal relationship between the leader, team, organization, and larger societal context. By understanding and embracing this interconnectedness, leaders can better navigate the complexities of their roles and drive positive, sustainable change in their organizations and beyond.

In an increasingly interconnected and complex world, leaders can no longer afford to operate with a narrow, isolated view of their decisions. Every action they take, every policy they implement, and every change they drive creates ripple effects that spread throughout their organizations and beyond. These effects extend not only across their immediate teams but also into broader organizational structures, external markets, societal dynamics, and even global systems. To navigate this complexity successfully, leaders must cultivate the ability to think in terms of systems—embracing a mindset that allows them to see the bigger picture and understand how various elements of their organization and the world around it are interconnected. This approach, known as *systems thinking*, is an essential skill for leaders who aim to make informed, sustainable decisions that account for both immediate outcomes and long-term impacts.

At its core, systems thinking is a way of understanding the world that focuses on relationships, patterns, and the interdependencies between different components of a larger whole. Rather than seeing an organization, a team, or a problem as a series of isolated elements, systems thinking encourages leaders to view these as part of a larger, dynamic system. Every part of this system influences and is influenced by, the others, creating a web of connections that must be understood holistically.

For leaders, this means recognizing that decisions made in one area of their organization can have far-reaching effects in other areas. A new strategy implemented in one department may improve efficiency there, but it could create unforeseen challenges in other parts of the organization. Similarly, leadership behaviors—whether positive or negative—cascade through teams, shaping organizational culture and affecting performance across multiple levels. Systems thinking encourages leaders to consider not only the direct outcomes of their decisions but also the secondary and tertiary effects that ripple throughout the system.

This perspective transforms leadership from a linear cause-and-effect process into a more nuanced and cyclical approach. Leaders who adopt systems thinking learn to anticipate the feedback loops, unintended consequences, and interconnected relationships that characterize complex systems. In doing so, they become more adept at managing complexity, driving change, and creating sustainable solutions that benefit the entire organization, not just individual parts of it.

Cultivating a systems thinking mindset requires leaders to expand their perspective, moving beyond short-term, isolated problem-solving and embracing a more holistic, long-term approach. This shift begins with several key practices that help leaders understand the full scope of their organization and the systems in which it operates.

The first step is for leaders to identify the system's components and relationships. Every organization comprises interrelated elements—people, processes, departments, and external stakeholders—that work together to achieve common goals. Systems thinkers start by mapping out these components and understanding how they interact. This involves asking questions like: How do the various teams and departments rely on each other? What processes connect different parts of the organization? How does external feedback—whether from customers, suppliers, or regulatory bodies—shape internal decision-making?

For example, a leader dealing with declining employee engagement might begin by mapping out all the factors contributing to workplace morale, from team dynamics and management styles to external stressors like industry pressures or changes in organizational policy. By looking at the system as a whole, rather than isolating one issue, the leader gains a more complete understanding of what needs to change.

Next, leaders must think in terms of interconnections and feedback loops. In a system, feedback loops occur when actions lead to outcomes that then influence future actions, creating cycles of cause and effect. Systems thinkers recognize that the decisions they make today will have consequences that feed back into the organization over time, sometimes in ways that are difficult to predict. Understanding these feedback loops helps leaders anticipate how short-term actions will play out in the long term.

For instance, consider a leader who decides to implement strict cost-cutting measures to improve the organization's financial position. While this decision might yield immediate savings, it could also create negative feedback loops if it reduces employee morale, limits investment in innovation, or damages the company's reputation. Systems thinkers weigh these potential long-term consequences alongside the short-term benefits, allowing them to make more informed decisions that balance immediate needs with future sustainability.

Anticipating unintended consequences is another critical aspect of systems thinking. In any complex system, decisions rarely have simple, isolated outcomes. Leaders must develop the ability to foresee how their actions might create unexpected ripple effects throughout the organization. This involves considering the potential secondary and tertiary impacts of their decisions, especially in areas that may not seem immediately connected.

For example, introducing new technology to improve efficiency might seem like a straightforward solution. However, systems thinkers would take the time to explore how this change could affect employee workflows, customer experiences, and even the organization's culture. Will employees need to be retrained? Will the new technology disrupt existing processes in ways that require adjustments elsewhere? Could it alienate certain stakeholders who prefer traditional methods? By thinking through these potential unintended consequences, systems-thinking leaders are better equipped to avoid negative outcomes and design more comprehensive and sustainable solutions.

Furthermore, systems thinking requires leaders to consider external and global influences. Organizations do not operate in isolation from the world around them. Market trends, technological advancements, economic conditions, and societal expectations all play a role in shaping the context in which leadership decisions are made. Leaders who embrace systems thinking stay attuned to these external forces, recognizing that their organization is part of a larger ecosystem of interconnected actors and forces.

In today's business landscape, issues such as environmental sustainability, corporate social responsibility, and social justice are no longer optional considerations—they are integral to how organizations are perceived by their customers, employees, and investors. A systems-thinking leader recognizes that decisions related to resource use, environmental impact, or social initiatives have far-reaching implications beyond the organization's immediate goals. They understand that these decisions can either strengthen the organization's reputation and long-term viability or expose it to risks from public backlash, regulatory penalties, or shifting market demands.

Finally, systems thinking encourages leaders to foster collaboration and cross-departmental thinking. Silos are the enemy of systems thinking. Leaders must break down these barriers by encouraging open communication and collaboration across teams, departments, and functions. This ensures that decisions made in one part of the organization consider the perspectives and needs of other areas, leading to more integrated and well-rounded solutions.

Leaders can create cross-departmental task forces to address organizational challenges that span multiple areas of expertise. This collaborative approach ensures that decisions are not made in isolation but are informed by a diversity of viewpoints and an understanding of how changes in one area might impact the system as a whole. By encouraging this kind of systems-wide thinking, leaders create a more cohesive organization where decisions are made with the entire system in mind.

The value of systems thinking for leaders becomes particularly clear when applied to real-world decision-making. Leaders who adopt this approach are better equipped to navigate the complexities of modern organizations, solve problems holistically, and lead change in a way that is both strategic and sustainable.

In strategic planning, systems-thinking leaders look beyond immediate goals to consider how their plans will unfold over time and across the entire organization. They recognize that short-term wins should align with long-term objectives and that the health of the system depends on balancing current needs with future growth. This broader perspective helps leaders make strategic choices resilient to change and disruption.

In problem-solving, systems thinking shifts the focus from quick fixes to root causes. Leaders analyze how problems are connected to broader systemic issues—such as communication breakdowns, misaligned incentives, or outdated processes—and design solutions that address these root causes rather than merely treating the symptoms. This approach leads to more sustainable problem-solving, where solutions are embedded in the system's overall functioning.

Regarding change management, systems-thinking leaders are particularly adept at guiding their organizations through transformation. They understand that changes in one part of the system will inevitably affect others, and they plan accordingly. By anticipating resistance, fostering collaboration, and aligning the organization's structures with its goals, systems-thinking leaders ensure that change is not only implemented but also sustained.

In sustainability initiatives, systems thinkers look at the long-term impact of their organization's operations on both internal and external ecosystems. They consider how decisions around resource use, environmental practices, and social responsibility will affect the organization's reputation, customer loyalty, and regulatory compliance. By thinking holistically, they create strategies that promote environmental stewardship, social responsibility, and financial sustainability.

Leaders who embrace systems thinking gain a significant advantage in navigating complexity, managing change, and fostering innovation.

This mindset allows them to:

Anticipate long-term impacts and unintended consequences, leading to more informed decision-making.

Break down silos and encourage collaboration across the organization, resulting in more integrated solutions.

Balance short-term needs with long-term objectives, ensuring the sustainability of their strategies.

Respond to external forces with agility and foresight, positioning their organizations to thrive in a dynamic global environment.

Ultimately, systems thinking transforms the way leaders approach their roles, enabling them to make decisions that are not only effective at the moment but also aligned with the broader, interconnected dynamics of their organizations and the world around them. This holistic perspective allows leaders to create lasting value, drive meaningful change, and build resilient organizations that thrive in an increasingly complex and interconnected world.

A powerful example of interconnected leadership comes from Unilever, a global consumer goods giant that has embraced a purpose-driven approach to business under the leadership of former CEO Paul Polman. Unilever's leadership strategy has been grounded in the belief that long-term business success is deeply intertwined with social and environmental sustainability. This vision is encapsulated in the company's Sustainable Living Plan, which aims to decouple Unilever's growth from its environmental footprint while increasing its positive social impact.

Polman's leadership exemplifies systems thinking. Early in his tenure, he boldly decided to stop providing quarterly earnings guidance, a move that signaled Unilever's shift from short-term financial performance to long-term sustainable growth. This decision reflected his belief that businesses must operate within planetary boundaries and that focusing solely on short-term profits would ultimately undermine Unilever's ability to thrive in the future.

Under Polman's leadership, Unilever embarked on ambitious sustainability initiatives, from reducing its carbon emissions and water usage to improving the livelihoods of smallholder farmers in its supply chain. By understanding the interconnectedness of environmental health, supply chain sustainability, and consumer trust, Unilever's leadership strategy created value across multiple dimensions.

Unilever's commitment to reducing the environmental impact of its products was not just a marketing ploy but a recognition of the growing consumer demand for sustainability. The company's leadership understood that its future depended on aligning its business practices with the values of a more environmentally conscious consumer base. As a result, Unilever introduced a range of eco-friendly products and launched initiatives like the "Sunlight Water Centers" in developing countries to improve access to clean water.

Unilever's interconnected leadership also extended to its supply chain. By investing in sustainable agriculture and fair labor practices, the company ensured that the farmers and communities who provide raw materials like palm oil and tea were not only treated fairly but also empowered to contribute to the company's long-term success. This holistic approach demonstrates how Unilever's leadership recognized the interdependencies between social responsibility, environmental stewardship, and business performance, creating a virtuous cycle of growth that benefits both the company and the world around it.

In the realm of social impact, the story of the Grameen Bank, founded by Nobel Peace Prize winner Muhammad Yunus, offers a compelling example of interconnected leadership that has transformed communities around the world. The Grameen Bank pioneered the concept of microfinance, offering small loans to impoverished individuals—primarily women—in rural areas to help them start businesses and improve their livelihoods. This leadership model is built on the recognition of the interdependence between economic empowerment, social equity, and community development.

Yunus's leadership at Grameen Bank was guided by the belief that providing financial resources to those who are typically excluded from traditional banking systems could lift entire communities out of poverty. Rather than viewing people with low incomes as untrustworthy or high-risk borrowers, Grameen Bank's leadership recognized the untapped potential within these communities and developed a system that leveraged social trust and peer accountability to ensure loan repayment.

The Grameen Bank's success is rooted in its understanding of the broader social systems in which it operates. By providing loans to women, the bank not only empowered individuals but also strengthened families and communities. The women who received loans were able to start small businesses, generate income, and improve their children's access to education and healthcare. This, in turn, contributed to the overall economic and social development of their communities, creating a ripple effect of positive change.

The Grameen Bank's leadership model demonstrated a deep understanding of the interconnectedness of economic development and social justice. By addressing the systemic barriers that kept marginalized communities trapped in poverty, Yunus and his team created a model that fostered sustainable development while challenging traditional notions of banking and finance.

The Grameen Bank's approach to leadership exemplifies how systems thinking and an understanding of interdependence can lead to innovative solutions that transform not only individual lives but also entire social structures. By recognizing that economic empowerment is deeply linked to social progress, Grameen Bank's leadership helped reshape the lives of millions of people around the world.

In the tech industry, Salesforce, under the leadership of CEO Marc Benioff, has become a model for interconnected leadership by embedding social responsibility into its business model. Salesforce's philosophy, known as the 1-1-1 model, dedicates 1% of its equity, 1% of its product, and 1% of its employees' time to philanthropic causes. This leadership approach acknowledges that Salesforce's success is not just measured by financial performance but by its contributions to society and its role in advancing positive change.

Benioff's leadership is based on the belief that businesses are responsible for giving back to the communities and systems that support them. Through its 1-1-1 model, Salesforce has donated millions of dollars, provided technology solutions to nonprofits, and empowered employees to engage in volunteer work. This interconnected approach to leadership reflects a deep understanding of how corporate success is linked to the health and well-being of society as a whole.

Salesforce's leadership also extends to its environmental initiatives. The company has committed to becoming a net-zero carbon company and is actively working to reduce its carbon footprint while advocating for greater environmental responsibility across the tech industry. By recognizing the interdependence between business success, environmental sustainability, and social equity, Salesforce's leadership exemplifies how organizations can thrive by embedding purpose and responsibility into their core operations.

Salesforce's approach demonstrates that interconnected leadership can drive both business growth and social impact. Benioff's leadership has not only positioned Salesforce as a leader in the tech industry but also as a champion for corporate responsibility, showing that companies can succeed while making meaningful contributions to the world around them.

Leaders who understand the systems in which they operate—whether those systems involve supply chains, social structures, environmental ecosystems, or global markets—are better equipped to make decisions that drive sustainable growth and create positive change.

Interconnected leadership is about recognizing that every decision, every action, has ripple effects that extend beyond immediate results. It is about seeing the bigger picture, understanding the interdependencies between business, society, and the environment, and leading with a mindset that embraces both short-term success and long-term responsibility. The stories of these organizations serve as powerful examples of how leaders who adopt a systems-thinking approach can create lasting value, foster innovation, and contribute to a more equitable and sustainable world.

Understanding the interconnectedness of leadership within a larger system requires more than just a theoretical grasp—it demands practical application. Leaders need tools and frameworks to help them visualize and manage the complex web of relationships, consequences, and dynamics that influence their decisions and the outcomes of their actions. Three powerful tools—Stakeholder Mapping, Decision Impact Analysis, and Feedback Loops—are designed to help leaders adopt a systems-thinking approach to their leadership. These tools enable leaders to see beyond immediate issues, understand the broader context in which they operate, and make informed decisions that account for both short-term and long-term effects across their organization and its surrounding environment.

Stakeholder Mapping ensures that leaders remain attuned to the needs and influence of key players within and outside their organizations. Decision Impact Analysis helps leaders foresee the ripple effects of their choices, allowing them to mitigate risks and maximize positive outcomes. Feedback Loops close the learning cycle, enabling leaders to adapt and iterate based on real-world outcomes.

Ultimately, these tools equip leaders with the ability to lead not just for today but for the future—building organizations that are resilient, adaptive, and sustainable in an ever-changing world.

Tool 1. Stakeholder Mapping: Visualizing the Web of Influence

What is Stakeholder Mapping?

Stakeholder Mapping is a tool that helps leaders identify and analyze the various individuals, groups, or entities that have a stake in the organization's decisions and actions. This tool allows leaders to visualize the network of relationships, both internal and external, that influence—and are influenced by—their leadership choices. Stakeholders can include employees, customers, suppliers, investors, regulators, communities, and even competitors, each of whom holds different interests, needs, and levels of influence.

By mapping out these stakeholders, leaders gain a clearer understanding of who is affected by their decisions, who holds the power to influence outcomes, and how various stakeholders interact with each other. This broader view helps leaders navigate the complex interdependencies within their organization and its environment, allowing them to make decisions that balance multiple interests and lead to more sustainable outcomes.

How to Use Stakeholder Mapping:

1. **Identify Your Stakeholders**: Begin by listing all the relevant stakeholders associated with your organization, project, or decision. These stakeholders can be internal (e.g., employees, managers, departments) and external (e.g., customers, suppliers, local communities, regulators, investors). Think broadly about anyone who may be affected by your decisions.

2. **Map Influence and Interest**: Once you have identified your stakeholders, map them according to their level of influence and interest in the organization or the decision at hand. Use a simple two-axis grid: one axis for the degree of influence (low to high) and one for the degree of interest (low to high). This allows you to visualize which stakeholders are most critical to engage and consider.

3. **Analyze Relationships and Interdependencies**: Consider how these stakeholders relate to one another and how their needs or concerns might overlap. Are there stakeholders with conflicting interests? Are some groups more dependent on the organization's decisions than others? By analyzing these relationships, you can better anticipate challenges, negotiate solutions, and address the needs of multiple groups simultaneously.

4. **Develop Engagement Strategies**: Based on your map, create strategies to engage key stakeholders, especially those with high influence and high interest. What can you do to address their needs or concerns? How can you involve them in decision-making to ensure alignment and buy-in?

Reflection and Benefits: Stakeholder Mapping encourages leaders to take a broader view of their organization's ecosystem, recognizing the diverse interests and power dynamics at play. By understanding how decisions impact various groups, leaders can make more informed, ethical, and sustainable choices that create long-term value for all involved.

Tool 2. Decision Impact Analysis: Anticipating the Ripple Effects

What is Decision Impact Analysis?

Decision Impact Analysis is a tool designed to help leaders systematically evaluate the potential consequences of their decisions, both intended and unintended. This tool helps leaders move beyond linear cause-and-effect thinking by examining how their choices might trigger ripple effects across the organization and beyond. It encourages leaders to think through the broader implications of their actions, considering not only immediate outcomes but also secondary and tertiary effects.

Using Decision Impact Analysis, leaders can identify potential risks, conflicts, and opportunities that may arise from their decisions. This tool fosters a proactive, rather than reactive, approach to leadership, allowing leaders to anticipate and mitigate negative consequences while maximizing positive outcomes.

How to Use Decision Impact Analysis:

1. **Define the Decision**: Start by clearly defining the decision you are analyzing. Be specific about what you are trying to achieve and the key objectives behind the decision. Consider whether the decision involves strategic direction, operational changes, personnel shifts, or resource allocation.

2. **Identify Direct Impacts**: List the immediate, direct impacts of the decision. Who or what will be directly affected by this choice? For example, a decision to implement new technology may directly affect IT teams, employees using the technology, and the budget allocated for training and development.

3. **Examine Secondary and Tertiary Effects**: Consider the indirect ripple effects that may follow from the direct impacts. How will these first-order changes affect other areas

of the organization or external stakeholders? For instance, implementing new technology might also impact customer experience, employee morale, or existing workflows. These secondary effects may lead to further consequences, such as changes in team dynamics or shifts in market perception.

4. **Consider Timing and Feedback Loops**: Some impacts may take time to materialize. Use Decision Impact Analysis to think about how the decision might unfold over time. Are there feedback loops that could amplify certain outcomes, either positively or negatively? For example, a new policy may improve efficiency in the short term but create burnout or disengagement over the long term if not carefully managed.

5. **Develop Contingency Plans**: Based on your analysis, identify potential risks and create contingency plans to address them. How will you monitor the outcomes of your decision, and what adjustments will you make if unintended consequences arise?

Reflection and Benefits: Decision Impact Analysis empowers leaders to make more thoughtful, strategic decisions by considering the broader implications of their actions. It encourages leaders to think holistically, accounting for not only the immediate benefits but also the long-term health of the organization and its stakeholders.

Tool 3. Feedback Loops: Creating Continuous Learning Cycles

What are Feedback Loops?

Feedback Loops are an essential tool for systems thinking, enabling leaders to create continuous learning cycles within their organization. A feedback loop is a process in which the outcomes of a decision or action are fed back into the system to influence future decisions. These loops can be either positive feedback loops that reinforce and amplify change or negative feedback loops that help regulate and stabilize a system by counteracting deviations.

Effective leaders understand that their decisions create feedback within the organization, and they use this feedback to refine their strategies, learn from outcomes, and make iterative improvements. By paying attention to both formal and informal feedback mechanisms—such as performance metrics, employee input, customer feedback, and market trends—leaders can adapt to changing conditions and ensure their organization remains resilient and responsive.

How to Use Feedback Loops:

1. **Identify Key Feedback Sources**: Start by identifying the various sources of feedback available to you. These could include performance data, customer satisfaction surveys, employee engagement scores, peer reviews, and financial metrics. Consider both quantitative and qualitative feedback sources that provide insight into how decisions are playing out.

2. **Establish Regular Feedback Mechanisms**: Create systems to capture feedback on an ongoing basis. This might involve setting up regular employee check-ins, running customer surveys, or reviewing key performance indicators (KPIs) on a monthly basis. Ensure that feedback is collected consistently and represents different parts of the organization.

3. **Analyze Feedback for Patterns**: Look for patterns and trends in the feedback you receive. Are certain issues repeatedly surfacing across multiple sources? Is there alignment between different feedback streams, or are there discrepancies? Analyzing these patterns will help you understand how decisions influence the broader system.

4. **Close the Loop with Action**: Feedback is only valuable if it leads to action. Once you have identified areas that need improvement or reinforcement, take steps to address them. Communicate changes to the relevant stakeholders, ensuring they understand how their input has been incorporated into future decisions.

5. **Monitor Long-Term Effects**: Feedback loops should not be one-time events; they are ongoing processes. Continuously monitor the outcomes of your decisions and gather new feedback to inform future actions. This creates a dynamic learning environment where leaders and organizations can evolve based on real-world experiences.

Reflection and Benefits: Feedback Loops provide leaders with the critical information they need to adapt and improve over time. By actively seeking feedback and integrating it into their decision-making processes, leaders foster a culture of continuous learning, innovation, and resilience.

Chapter 5
Ethical Leadership as a Moral Imperative

True leadership lies not just in the ability to inspire others or drive results but also in a deep commitment to ethics and integrity. Ethical leadership is foundational to unlocking infinite potential in oneself, in others, and organizations as a whole. It provides the moral compass that guides every decision and ensures that actions align with values. For leaders, this means balancing visionary goals with a steadfast dedication to ethical responsibility, ensuring that success is achieved not only in the short term but in a way that is sustainable, fair, and principled.

In a world where decisions often carry far-reaching consequences, leaders are frequently faced with complex choices that require more than just strategic thinking. They must navigate these decisions with a clear sense of moral responsibility, understanding that the pursuit of growth, profit, or innovation must never come at the cost of integrity. Ethical leadership demands that vision is not merely aspirational but is built on a foundation of trust, transparency, and accountability. Leaders who embrace this principle unlock not only their own potential but also foster an environment where others can thrive, innovate, and grow within a framework of shared values.

Visionary leaders often push the boundaries of what is possible, encouraging their teams and organizations to strive for greatness, embrace bold ideas, and pursue ambitious goals. However, vision without integrity can be dangerous. When leaders are focused solely on achieving their vision, they risk making decisions that compromise their values or harm others in the process. This can lead to short-term gains but long-term damage to the leader's reputation, the organization's culture, and the trust that stakeholders place in them.

Ethical leadership requires leaders to balance their visionary aspirations with a commitment to doing what is right. It means that leaders are willing to sacrifice short-term benefits if it means upholding ethical standards and acting with integrity. For instance, a company might have the opportunity to cut costs by compromising on product quality or labor standards. A visionary leader driven solely by profit might be tempted to take this shortcut, but an ethical leader understands that such actions, while beneficial in the short term, could undermine trust with customers, damage brand reputation, and harm the company in the long run.

Integrity in leadership is not about avoiding difficult decisions but about ensuring that every decision is made with a clear sense of responsibility to those affected. This includes employees, customers, partners, and even society at large. Leaders must be able to envision not just what success looks like but also how to achieve it in a way that aligns with the ethical values of the organization. This kind of leadership fosters an environment where people feel safe, valued, and motivated to contribute their best because they trust that their leaders are acting with integrity.

Ethical leadership is not just about avoiding scandals or negative consequences—it is about creating sustainable success. When leaders consistently act with integrity, they build trust with their teams, stakeholders, and the broader public. Trust is a critical asset in any organization and cannot be bought or manufactured. It must be earned through consistent, ethical behavior. Once established, trust allows leaders to inspire loyalty, foster collaboration, and create a culture where innovation and risk-taking are encouraged because people know that their leaders have their best interests at heart.

Ethical leadership contributes to long-term success by promoting accountability. Leaders who hold themselves and others accountable for ethical behavior set a standard for the entire organization. They create systems and structures that ensure transparency, fairness, and equity in decision-making. This leads to better outcomes, as decisions are not made in silos or based on short-term thinking but are evaluated through the lens of long-term impact and ethical responsibility.

One of the most significant benefits of ethical leadership is that it cultivates a culture of integrity within the organization. When employees see their leaders consistently making principled decisions, they are more likely to adopt similar values in their own work. This creates a ripple effect, where ethical behavior becomes embedded in the organization's DNA, influencing everything from day-to-day operations to high-level strategic decisions. Over time, this culture of integrity not only enhances the organization's reputation but also contributes to its long-term resilience and adaptability.

Unlocking infinite potential is impossible without a strong ethical foundation. Leaders who prioritize ethical decision-making empower others to do the same. This creates a virtuous cycle, where individuals feel trusted and empowered to take initiative, take risks, and think creatively—all within a framework of accountability and integrity. Ethical leadership opens the door for innovation by providing the psychological safety necessary for individuals to explore new ideas without fear of retaliation or unethical repercussions.

Ethical leaders understand that their role extends beyond the confines of their organization. They recognize that their actions have ripple effects throughout society, influencing not only the people within their immediate sphere but also the communities and industries in which they operate. This awareness of the broader system is crucial for leaders who seek to unlock infinite potential in themselves and others. By acting with integrity and considering the wider impact of their decisions, leaders contribute to the creation of systems and structures that support sustainable growth and positive social change.

Leaders in industries such as technology or finance wield significant influence over the direction of society. Their decisions regarding data privacy, labor practices, or environmental sustainability have far-reaching consequences. Ethical leaders in these fields are not only tasked with driving innovation and profitability but also with ensuring that their actions do not exacerbate social inequities or environmental degradation. When these leaders balance their vision for the future with ethical responsibility, they unlock potential not only within their organizations but also in the wider world.

Ethical leadership is not without its challenges. Leaders are often faced with situations where the "right" decision is not immediately clear, or where ethical principles come into conflict with business objectives. In such cases, leaders must rely on their moral compass, seek counsel from trusted advisors, and be willing to engage in difficult conversations about values and trade-offs.

Ethical leadership often requires courage. Leaders may face pressure from shareholders, investors, or competitors to make decisions that prioritize short-term gains over long-term ethical considerations. Standing firm in one's ethical convictions, even when it means sacrificing immediate rewards, is a hallmark of true leadership. It is this commitment to doing what is right, regardless of external pressures, that allows leaders to maintain their integrity and, in the long run, achieve success that is both meaningful and sustainable.

At the core of unlocking infinite potential is the understanding that leadership must be built on a foundation of ethics and integrity. Vision without ethical grounding can lead to unsustainable, short-lived success that ultimately erodes trust and damages the very systems it seeks to improve. Conversely, when leaders balance their visionary goals with long-term ethical responsibility, they create the conditions for sustained growth, innovation, and positive impact.

Ethical leadership empowers individuals, strengthens organizations, and contributes to a more just and equitable world. It is the foundation upon which infinite potential is realized, ensuring that the path to success is not only achievable but also meaningful, enduring, and aligned with the greater good. Leaders who embrace this responsibility unlock their own potential and the collective potential of everyone they lead.

Throughout history, there have been leaders who have not only driven extraordinary success within their organizations but also done so while adhering to the highest ethical standards. These leaders have demonstrated that success and ethics are not mutually exclusive. In fact, they have shown that leading with integrity can result in more sustainable, impactful, and lasting change. Whether in business, politics, social enterprises, or activism, these individuals have shaped their industries and left a legacy defined not only by what they achieved but by how they achieved it.

Dr. Paul Farmer was a pioneering physician, anthropologist, and co-founder of Partners In Health (PIH), an organization dedicated to providing quality healthcare to impoverished populations around the world. Farmer's leadership was grounded in a deep ethical commitment to health equity, particularly for those in regions most affected by poverty and lack of access to healthcare. His vision of healthcare was not limited to technical solutions but was infused with a moral imperative to treat all human beings with dignity, regardless of their socioeconomic status.

Farmer's work began in rural Haiti in the 1980s, where he set up a clinic in Cange, a remote village suffering from extreme poverty. He provided healthcare services that rivaled those available in the world's wealthiest countries, challenging the idea that high-quality care should be reserved for the privileged. His approach to leadership was holistic, focusing on addressing the social determinants of health—such as education, housing, clean water, and food security—alongside medical treatment.

Farmer's ethical leadership extended beyond clinical care to policy advocacy. He championed healthcare as a human right, influencing global institutions like the World Health Organization (WHO) and the United Nations to prioritize health equity. His tireless efforts against diseases like tuberculosis, HIV/AIDS, and Ebola in underserved communities showcased how leadership could blend scientific rigor with deep ethical responsibility.

Through PIH, Farmer created a new model of global healthcare that remains a gold standard for ethical leadership in the field of medicine and public health. His legacy is one of compassion, equity, and relentless pursuit of justice for the world's poorest populations.

Eileen Fisher, the founder of the eponymous Eileen Fisher fashion brand, redefined the fashion industry through her ethical leadership in sustainable fashion. At a time when fast fashion was becoming the dominant model, Fisher built her company on the principles of environmental responsibility, fair labor practices, and conscious capitalism. She believed that business success should not come at the expense of the planet or people and that fashion could be both beautiful and sustainable.

From the very beginning, Fisher's leadership style was collaborative and inclusive, fostering a culture of shared values within her company. She pioneered practices such as transparent supply chains, where the sources of materials and the conditions in which they were produced were known and verified. The company was one of the first in the industry to use organic cotton and non-toxic dyes long before these practices became fashionable.

Beyond the environmental aspects, Fisher's ethical leadership was also focused on the empowerment of workers. Her company advocated for fair wages, safe working conditions, and the economic empowerment of women. She structured her company to reflect her commitment to ethics, even establishing a profit-sharing model for employees to ensure that success was shared across the organization.

Fisher's influence extended beyond her own brand. She became a vocal advocate for sustainability and ethical practices in fashion, working to raise awareness about the negative impacts of fast fashion and promoting more responsible consumption. By combining environmental stewardship with human rights advocacy, Eileen Fisher's leadership stands as a powerful example of how business success can be aligned with a greater moral and ethical responsibility.

Jacqueline Novogratz, founder and CEO of Acumen, revolutionized the world of philanthropy and impact investing through her ethical leadership and dedication to fighting global poverty. Acumen is a nonprofit impact investment fund that uses patient capital to invest in social enterprises, providing long-term financial support to businesses that address the needs of low-income communities. Novogratz's approach to leadership was centered on the belief that dignity, not dependence, is what transforms poverty and that markets could be leveraged ethically to drive positive social change.

Novogratz founded Acumen in 2001, driven by a desire to challenge the traditional philanthropic model, which she saw as limited in its ability to drive systemic change. Instead, she sought to invest in innovative entrepreneurs who were working on solutions to critical issues like clean water access, affordable healthcare, education, and energy for underserved populations. Her leadership emphasized the importance of holding both investors and entrepreneurs accountable to ethical standards that prioritize human dignity over financial returns.

Her approach to ethical leadership was innovative in the way it merged the worlds of business and philanthropy. Novogratz argued that impact investing was not just about making a profit while doing good—it was about fundamentally reshaping how markets operate to serve humanity's greatest needs. Acumen's investments were made with a long-term perspective, recognizing that transformative social change requires patience, resilience, and commitment.

By fostering a network of social entrepreneurs who are deeply committed to ethical principles, Novogratz has created a model of leadership that challenges the status quo in both business and philanthropy. Her leadership at Acumen demonstrates that ethical investment strategies can unlock innovation and entrepreneurial spirit in some of the world's most disadvantaged regions.

Ellen Johnson Sirleaf, the first female president of Liberia and Africa's first elected female head of state, is a global symbol of ethical, political leadership. Her presidency, which lasted from 2006 to 2018, followed a devastating civil war, and Sirleaf inherited a country ravaged by conflict, corruption, and poverty. Despite these challenges, she pursued a leadership style rooted in integrity, accountability, and a vision for rebuilding Liberia through democratic governance and economic reforms.

Sirleaf's ethical leadership was evident from the start of her presidency. She made the fight against corruption one of her primary goals, recognizing that entrenched corruption had eroded public trust in government and stymied development. She implemented sweeping reforms in public financial management, ensuring transparency in government spending and accountability for leaders who misused public funds. These efforts earned her international recognition, including the Nobel Peace Prize in 2011, which she shared for her nonviolent struggle for women's safety and rights.

Under Sirleaf's leadership, Liberia began to recover from decades of conflict, and her administration attracted significant foreign investment by emphasizing good governance and the rule of law. She was deeply committed to empowering women, advocating for their increased participation in politics and public life, and supporting initiatives aimed at improving education and healthcare for women and children.

Despite significant challenges, including the Ebola epidemic that hit Liberia during her presidency, Sirleaf's ethical leadership helped stabilize Liberia's economy and rebuild its democratic institutions. Her presidency stands as a testament to the power of ethical governance in the political sphere, where principled leadership can lay the groundwork for national healing and long-term development.

Hamdi Ulukaya, the founder and CEO of Chobani, revolutionized the food industry by building a billion-dollar company with ethics at the core of its business model. Ulukaya, an immigrant from Turkey, transformed a failing yogurt factory in upstate New York into one of the most successful yogurt brands in the United States. But beyond Chobani's financial success, what sets Ulukaya apart as an ethical leader is his commitment to creating a business that prioritizes social responsibility, employee well-being, and community impact.

Ulukaya's leadership at Chobani is characterized by his deep concern for workers' rights and his belief that business should be a force for good. One of his most notable initiatives was giving 10% of Chobani's shares to its employees, ensuring that the company's success would be shared by those who helped build it. This decision was not just a financial gesture; it reflected Ulukaya's belief that workers should be treated as partners and that businesses have a moral obligation to uplift their employees.

In addition to his commitment to employee welfare, Ulukaya has been a vocal advocate for refugees. In 2016, he launched the Tent Partnership for Refugees, a nonprofit organization that mobilizes the business community to improve the lives of refugees through job opportunities and economic integration. Chobani itself employs hundreds of refugees and immigrants, providing them with a chance to rebuild their lives and contribute to their communities.

Ulukaya's ethical leadership has helped redefine what it means to be a successful CEO in the 21st century. His focus on people, social impact, and shared prosperity has not only driven Chobani's growth but also set an example for other business leaders to follow. His belief in ethical capitalism—where profits and social good can go hand in hand—continues to inspire a new generation of socially conscious entrepreneurs.

Malala Yousafzai is best known for her extraordinary courage in advocating for girls' education, but her leadership goes far beyond personal bravery. Malala's ethical leadership has inspired a global movement, demonstrating how an individual's commitment to justice and equality can galvanize change on a worldwide scale.

At the age of fifteen, Malala was shot by the Taliban for her outspoken advocacy for girls' education in Pakistan. After surviving the attack, she became a global symbol for the fight against oppression and the right to education for all children, particularly girls. Her leadership is grounded in a deep moral conviction that education is a fundamental human right, and she has used her platform to call attention to the millions of girls around the world who are denied this right.

Malala co-founded the Malala Fund, an organization dedicated to ensuring every girl receives 12 years of free, safe, and quality education. Through her advocacy, she has influenced policymakers, engaged world leaders, and mobilized young people.

Leadership is not simply about reaching organizational goals, driving innovation, or achieving personal success. True leadership embodies responsibility at its core—especially the responsibility to ensure that one's actions contribute positively to the broader social good. In a world where leaders influence not only their teams but also larger societal, economic, and environmental structures, this responsibility has never been more crucial. Leadership's moral imperative demands that decisions made by those in power benefit more than just the immediate stakeholders. It is about considering long-term impacts, upholding ethical principles, and creating lasting, positive change that serves humanity and future generations.

The notion of moral imperatives in leadership stems from the belief that with influence comes an obligation to act for the greater good. Leaders, by virtue of their roles, have the power to shape their organizations and communities. This influence brings the responsibility to make decisions that go beyond personal or financial gain and instead prioritize fairness, sustainability, and justice. To lead effectively in today's complex, interconnected world, leaders must embrace the challenge of making decisions that balance organizational goals with broader social, environmental, and ethical concerns. Let us explore how leaders can embrace moral imperatives to ensure their actions create meaningful, positive change.

The first step for any leader committed to moral responsibility is developing a heightened awareness of how their decisions impact not only their immediate organization but also the world beyond it. Leadership cannot be confined to internal matters; it must extend into the broader social, environmental, and economic realms. Leaders must regularly ask themselves fundamental questions to ensure they are acting in the best interests of the broader system:

Who will be affected by this decision? Leaders should consider not just their employees, shareholders, or customers but also external stakeholders, such as the communities they operate in, the environment, and even future generations. For example, a decision to streamline production may reduce costs in the short term but could result in job losses, environmental harm, or compromised product quality. Ethical leaders examine these ripple effects, understanding that their decisions impact a wide range of people and systems, often in unexpected ways.

What are the long-term consequences? Ethical leadership demands a forward-looking perspective. While short-term gains are often appealing, leaders must consider the sustainability of their actions over time. Decisions that bring immediate success but create long-term harm—such as environmental degradation, deepening social inequities, or eroding trust—are ethically problematic. True ethical leadership involves balancing the needs of today with the responsibilities of tomorrow, ensuring that decisions contribute to the long-term well-being of all stakeholders.

How does this align with the values of social justice and equity? Ethical leadership is also about promoting fairness and opportunity. Leaders must be conscious of whether their actions are contributing to social justice or exacerbating existing inequalities. Are they creating pathways for inclusion, promoting diversity, and ensuring that opportunities are available to those who have historically been marginalized? Ethical leaders actively work to build systems that are more just and equitable, ensuring that their success is shared and their impact is positive.

For leaders to truly fulfill their moral obligations, social responsibility cannot be limited to isolated initiatives or occasional charitable actions. Instead, it must be embedded into the core values and daily practices of the organization. This ensures that the commitment to the broader social good is not temporary or reactive but a fundamental part of how the organization operates. Ethical leadership must become a lived practice across all levels of the organization.

One way to achieve this is by creating a mission that reflects a social purpose. A strong, purpose-driven mission statement anchors the organization in a broader sense of responsibility. Leaders should ensure that their mission goes beyond profits and operational goals, explicitly acknowledging a commitment to societal impact. Whether through environmental sustainability efforts, social equity initiatives, or ethical sourcing practices, the mission should serve as a guiding principle for every decision the organization makes.

Leaders must also operationalize ethical standards. It is not enough to articulate values—those values must be translated into concrete policies and actions. This includes ensuring that business practices reflect the organization's ethical commitments, from supply chain management to employee relations. For instance, a company that values environmental sustainability should implement measures to reduce waste, minimize carbon emissions, and adopt eco-friendly production methods. Likewise, a company that values equity should have clear policies on fair wages, inclusive hiring practices, and employee development opportunities. Embedding these ethical standards into the organization's operations ensures that moral imperatives are not just theoretical ideals but lived values.

Engaging in meaningful corporate social responsibility (CSR) initiatives is another way for leaders to contribute to the broader good. However, these initiatives should not be treated as afterthoughts or public relations exercises. Ethical leaders ensure that CSR is integrated into their business model in a way that aligns with their values and makes a tangible, positive impact on society. For instance, companies can invest in initiatives that address pressing societal issues, such as reducing carbon footprints, improving access to education, or supporting local communities. By doing so, they contribute to long-term social change while reinforcing their ethical leadership.

To ensure that moral imperatives are embedded into an organization's culture, leaders must model the values they espouse. Ethical leadership is about setting an example through actions, not just words. When leaders consistently demonstrate integrity, transparency, and social responsibility, they set the tone for the entire organization, making it clear that ethical behavior is the standard.

Prioritizing transparency and honesty is one of the most powerful ways a leader can model ethical behavior. Leaders must be open about their decision-making processes, especially when facing challenging or ethically complex situations. Transparency fosters trust both within the organization and with external stakeholders, ensuring that all parties feel confident in the leader's integrity. When decisions are transparent, stakeholders can see that the leader has considered multiple perspectives and weighed the ethical implications of their choices.

Another critical aspect of modeling ethical behavior is standing firm on ethical principles, even when doing so may be difficult or unpopular. There will inevitably be times when leaders are pressured to compromise their values in pursuit of short-term gains—whether through cutting corners, bypassing regulations, or sacrificing long-term ethical commitments for immediate rewards. Ethical leaders must have the moral courage to resist these pressures and remain steadfast in their commitment to integrity. This courage demonstrates that ethical principles are non-negotiable and that long-term success must be built on a foundation of trust and responsibility.

Fostering a culture of accountability is also essential for ensuring that moral imperatives are upheld throughout the organization. Leaders who hold themselves and others accountable for ethical behavior create an environment where ethical lapses are identified and addressed. This might involve creating systems for reporting unethical behavior, instituting internal ethics committees, or establishing channels for feedback and transparency. By building a culture of accountability, leaders ensure that ethical principles are consistently enforced, reinforcing the organization's commitment to the greater good.

In the 21st century, one of the most urgent moral imperatives for leaders is addressing environmental sustainability. The environmental challenges facing the world today—from climate change to resource depletion—are immense, and leaders must recognize their responsibility to mitigate harm and promote sustainable practices. Ethical leadership in this context requires more than just complying with regulations; it demands a proactive commitment to preserving the environment for future generations.

Ethical leaders must commit to sustainable practices that reduce their organization's environmental footprint. This might involve transitioning to renewable energy, minimizing waste, adopting circular economy principles, or implementing eco-friendly sourcing practices. Sustainability should not be an afterthought or a secondary concern—it should be central to the organization's strategy, reflecting a long-term commitment to the well-being of the planet.

Leaders must also incorporate climate resilience into their business strategies. Forward-thinking leaders recognize that environmental changes will continue to shape the business landscape in the coming decades. As such, they integrate climate resilience into their planning, ensuring that their organizations are prepared for the risks posed by climate change while continuing to contribute to sustainable development. By doing so, they not only protect their businesses but also contribute to broader efforts to combat environmental degradation.

Ethical leaders understand that their responsibility extends beyond their own organization. They use their influence to advocate for industry-wide change, pushing for higher environmental standards and collective action on issues like deforestation, pollution, and biodiversity loss. By leading by example and calling for greater accountability across industries, ethical leaders help create a broader cultural shift toward more responsible and sustainable economic systems.

At the heart of moral leadership is the concept of stewardship. Ethical leaders view their role not as one of personal gain or accumulation of power but as a temporary custodianship of resources, influence, and responsibility. As stewards, leaders recognize that their decisions must prioritize the well-being of future generations, ensuring that the systems they manage today are left in a better state than when they took charge.

One of the most critical aspects of stewardship is investing in human capital. Ethical leaders understand that their greatest responsibility is to the people they lead. This means creating opportunities for growth, providing fair compensation, fostering an inclusive work environment, and ensuring that employees are treated with dignity and respect. Leaders who invest in their people are not only enhancing organizational performance but are also contributing to the broader social good by improving economic mobility, job satisfaction, and employee well-being.

Beyond their immediate responsibilities, ethical leaders often use their platforms to support broader social causes. Whether advocating for human rights, advancing gender equality, promoting education, or supporting public health, these leaders recognize that their influence can drive meaningful change on a societal level. By speaking out on critical issues and supporting initiatives that promote justice, equity, and opportunity, leaders extend their ethical responsibility beyond their organizations and into the broader world.

Moral imperatives are not abstract concepts—they are the guiding principles that shape every decision ethical leaders make. True leadership requires an unwavering commitment to ensuring that decisions contribute positively to the broader social good. This means considering the long-term impact of every action, prioritizing sustainability, fostering accountability, and investing in people.

Ethical leadership is about creating value not just for shareholders or employees but for society as a whole. Leaders who embrace their moral imperatives unlock the potential for meaningful, lasting change, both within their organizations and in the world around them. In a time when the consequences of leadership decisions are more far-reaching than ever, leaders must rise to the challenge, using their influence not for personal gain but for the greater good—ensuring that their legacy is one of integrity, responsibility, and positive impact.

Making ethical decisions as a leader requires more than intuition or good intentions; it demands a structured approach to ensure that choices align with both personal values and organizational ethics. Leaders frequently face complex situations where the right course of action is unclear, multiple stakeholders have competing interests, or short-term pressures challenge long-term ethical commitments. To navigate these challenges effectively, leaders must rely on ethical decision-making frameworks and engage in reflective exercises that deepen their self-awareness and commitment to moral integrity.

Ethical leadership is a continuous journey that requires commitment, self-awareness, and practical tools to navigate complex dilemmas. By integrating ethical decision-making frameworks, practical tools like the Values Alignment Chart and Stakeholder Impact Assessment, and reflective exercises, leaders can ensure their decisions align with both personal and organizational ethics. These practices help leaders stay grounded in their values, make thoughtful and responsible decisions, and foster a culture of integrity within their organizations. Through consistent application, leaders can build trust, accountability, and long-term success while contributing positively to the broader social good.

The Ethical Decision-Making Framework: A Step-by-Step Guide

One of the most effective ways to approach complex ethical decisions is through a structured framework that guides leaders through a series of critical questions. This framework helps ensure that decisions are not made impulsively or based solely on short-term factors but are grounded in thoughtful consideration of the ethical implications.

Step 1: Clarify the Ethical Dilemma

The first step in ethical decision-making is to clearly define the ethical dilemma. Ethical dilemmas often arise when values, responsibilities, or stakeholder interests conflict. In this step, leaders must ask:

- What is the specific issue or decision that needs to be made?

- Who are the stakeholders involved, and how will they be impacted by the decision?

- What are the competing values or priorities at stake (e.g., fairness, transparency, profitability, sustainability)?

For example, a company may face an ethical dilemma when deciding whether to outsource production to a country with lower labor costs but questionable labor practices. The tension between cost efficiency and fair labor standards creates a dilemma that must be carefully considered.

Step 2: Gather Information and Evaluate Alternatives

Once the dilemma is defined, the next step is to gather all relevant information and explore possible alternatives. Leaders should assess the facts of the situation, understand the potential consequences of each course of action, and consider how these alternatives align with ethical principles. Key questions include:

- What are the possible courses of action?

- What are the likely outcomes of each alternative, both in the short and long term?

- How do these alternatives align with the organization's values, mission, and ethical commitments?

For instance, in the outsourcing scenario, the leader might explore alternatives such as working only with certified ethical suppliers or investing in local job creation instead of outsourcing to a lower-cost region with poor labor standards.

Step 3: Evaluate the Decision through Ethical Lenses

This step is crucial for ensuring that the decision aligns with ethical standards. Leaders should examine the decision through various ethical lenses, such as:

- **Utilitarian Approach**: What decision will produce the greatest good for the greatest number of people?

- **Deontological Approach**: What is the leader's duty or obligation in this situation, regardless of the consequences?

- **Virtue Ethics**: What decision is consistent with the leader's character and the virtues they aim to embody (e.g., honesty, fairness, integrity)?

- **Justice Approach**: What decision is the most fair and equitable for all stakeholders?

Applying these different ethical frameworks helps leaders balance competing interests and choose a course of action that is consistent with their ethical commitments.

Step 4: Make the Decision and Take Responsibility

After evaluating the options and their ethical implications, the leader must make a decision. This step requires the leader to be confident in their ethical reasoning and take responsibility for the outcomes. Leaders must ask themselves:

- Am I willing to take full responsibility for this decision, including its consequences for all stakeholders?

- How will I communicate this decision transparently to those affected?

- Does this decision reflect the values I want to uphold both personally and for the organization?

Once a decision is made, it is essential that leaders communicate it clearly and explain the reasoning behind it, especially in situations where stakeholders may disagree with the outcome. Transparent communication builds trust and demonstrates that the decision was made with integrity and consideration.

Step 5: Reflect on the Decision and Learn

Ethical decision-making is an ongoing process, and leaders should continually reflect on their decisions to learn from them. After the decision has been implemented, leaders can engage in reflective exercises to assess how the decision aligned with their values and what they can learn from the experience. Key reflective questions include:

- Did the decision achieve the desired ethical outcome?

- What were the unintended consequences, if any, and how were they addressed?

- What did I learn from this situation that will inform future ethical decisions?

Reflection helps leaders grow in their ethical leadership by learning from both their successes and their challenges.

Tool 1. The Values Alignment Chart

The Values Alignment Chart is a tool that helps leaders align their personal values with organizational values when making decisions. This tool is particularly useful when a leader's personal convictions may become tension with business objectives. The chart provides a structured way to identify and compare core values, ensuring that the decision-making process honors both personal and organizational ethics.

How to Use the Values Alignment Chart:

- List your personal core values (e.g., integrity, fairness, transparency).

- List the core values of the organization (e.g., innovation, sustainability, inclusivity).

- For each potential decision, evaluate how it aligns with both sets of values.

- Identify areas of conflict or tension and explore how they can be resolved through compromise or creative problem-solving.

This exercise fosters greater alignment between the leader's personal ethics and the organization's mission, ensuring that decisions are made with integrity.

Tool 2. Stakeholder Impact Assessment

The Stakeholder Impact Assessment is a tool designed to help leaders consider the broader social, environmental, and economic impact of their decisions on various stakeholder groups. This tool is particularly effective for ensuring that leaders take a systemic, long-term view of their ethical responsibilities.

Steps for Stakeholder Impact Assessment:

- Identify the primary and secondary stakeholders affected by the decision (e.g., employees, customers, suppliers, local communities, and environmental ecosystems).

- For each stakeholder group, assess the potential positive and negative impacts of the decision.

- Consider both short-term and long-term effects and weigh the ethical considerations of each impact.

- Identify mitigation strategies for minimizing negative impacts and enhancing positive outcomes.

The Stakeholder Impact Assessment ensures that leaders take a holistic view of their decisions, considering how their actions will affect not only direct stakeholders but also the broader community and environment.

Tool 3. The Ethical Decision Checklist

The Ethical Decision Checklist is a simple yet powerful tool that helps leaders ensure they are making decisions in line with ethical principles. Before making any significant decision, leaders can run through the checklist to confirm they have considered all relevant ethical factors.

The Ethical Decision Checklist:

- Is this decision legal and compliant with all relevant regulations?

- Does this decision align with both my personal values and the organization's values?

- Have I considered the potential long-term impacts on all stakeholders, including marginalized groups?

- Am I being transparent about my decision-making process?

- Will I feel comfortable and proud to stand by this decision if it becomes public knowledge?

- Have I sought input from diverse perspectives to ensure a well-rounded decision?

This checklist can serve as a final safeguard before making decisions, helping leaders ensure they are acting with integrity and accountability.

Exercise 1. The Values Reflection Journal

The Values Reflection Journal is a personal tool for leaders to regularly reflect on how their actions align with their core values. By setting aside time to journal after significant decisions or challenges, leaders can gain insights into their ethical leadership journey.

How to Use the Values Reflection Journal:

- After making a significant decision, write about how the decision aligned with your personal values.

- Reflect on any ethical challenges you encountered and how you addressed them.

- Consider what you learned from the decision and how it will shape your future leadership.

- Identify areas where you may have compromised your values and explore how you can address these challenges in the future.

This practice fosters self-awareness and encourages leaders to continuously refine their ethical decision-making skills.

Exercise 2. The Ethical Leadership Self-Assessment

The Ethical Leadership Self-Assessment is a structured exercise that allows leaders to evaluate their performance in adhering to ethical principles over time. By regularly engaging in self-assessment, leaders can identify areas of strength and areas for improvement.

Steps for the Ethical Leadership Self-Assessment:

- Reflect on recent decisions and assess how well they aligned with ethical principles such as fairness, transparency, and accountability.

- Identify any situations where you felt conflicted or uncertain about the ethical course of action and analyze how you handled those situations.

- Ask for feedback from trusted colleagues or mentors on your ethical leadership and incorporate their perspectives into your self-assessment.

- Set goals for improving your ethical leadership and identify specific actions you will take to meet those goals.

By regularly assessing their ethical performance, leaders can grow in their moral leadership and ensure that their actions consistently align with their values.

Chapter 6
Leading for the Long Game

In an age where instant gratification and immediate results often dominate the narrative of success, the most impactful and enduring leaders are those who resist the pull of short-termism. Instead, they cultivate a vision that transcends immediate gains, focusing on the long-term impact of their decisions and actions. These leaders recognize that true success is not measured by the achievements of today, but by the legacy, they leave behind—the sustainable growth, the empowered teams, and the societal contributions that outlast their tenure. This long-term perspective is a hallmark of ethical, visionary leadership.

Short-term results, while tempting, can lead leaders to make decisions that maximize immediate performance at the expense of future stability. Whether driven by quarterly earnings, rapid market gains, or quick wins in leadership positions, the pressure for immediate outcomes can often blind leaders to the larger picture. A short-term mindset might sacrifice the pillars sustaining long-term success: trust, innovation, employee engagement, and organizational culture. Great leaders understand that these foundational elements are not built overnight and that focusing solely on the present can undermine the future.

Leaders who prioritize short-term gains often do so under pressure—pressure from shareholders, stakeholders, market trends, or even their own desire for validation. The allure of hitting financial targets or securing a quick victory in a leadership challenge can be overwhelming. However, decisions based solely on short-term considerations can have significant negative consequences, both for the organization and its broader ecosystem.

For example, cutting costs by reducing employee development programs or scaling back on innovation initiatives may improve the bottom line in the immediate term, but over time, these decisions erode the organization's talent base and capacity for future growth. Similarly, prioritizing quick profits by overlooking ethical considerations—such as environmental impact or labor practices—can damage the organization's reputation, leading to long-term brand erosion and a loss of trust with consumers and stakeholders.

Great leaders avoid these traps by taking a more holistic view of leadership, recognizing that short-term gains are often fleeting, while long-term impact shapes the future of the organization and society. They understand that today's decisions must be made with tomorrow in mind, and they are willing to sacrifice immediate gratification for sustainable success.

Focusing on long-term impact requires leaders to be patient, strategic, and resilient. It means cultivating a vision that stretches beyond the current quarter, fiscal year, or project cycle. Great leaders are not just concerned with what they can accomplish during their time in leadership but also with how their decisions will influence the organization and its people in the years and decades to come.

Leaders with a long-term perspective understand that building a strong organizational culture, fostering innovation, and nurturing talent takes time. They invest in their people, knowing that empowered, engaged employees will drive the organization forward in the future. They encourage innovation and risk-taking, even if the results may not materialize immediately, because they know that innovation is the key to long-term competitiveness. These leaders are also deeply aware of their responsibility to leave behind a healthier, more resilient organization than the one they inherited.

A clear example of long-term leadership comes from companies that have built their success on sustainable practices. These organizations, led by visionary leaders, recognize that business growth does not have to come at the expense of environmental or social well-being. By adopting sustainable models that prioritize the long-term health of the planet, these leaders ensure that their businesses will continue to thrive in a world increasingly focused on ecological and social responsibility.

Great leaders also understand that the true measure of leadership lies not in their personal achievements but in the legacy they leave behind. While short-term results may bring recognition or financial rewards, they are fleeting in comparison to the lasting impact of a well-built legacy. A legacy is about more than just financial performance—it is about the relationships cultivated, the culture shaped, and the long-term contributions made to society.

For leaders who focus on legacy, their goal is not to be the person remembered for a single victory or achievement but to be the one who set in motion the forces that propelled the organization or community toward lasting success. This could involve establishing a culture of integrity, mentoring the next generation of leaders, or creating systems that enable sustainable growth for decades to come. These leaders are focused on building organizations that can thrive independently of their personal leadership, ensuring continuity and resilience even after they have stepped down.

One of the greatest challenges of leading with a long-term vision is resisting the constant pressure for immediate results. The modern business landscape, with its quarterly earnings reports, constant market fluctuations, and intense competition, often pushes leaders toward short-term thinking. Investors, boards, and even employees may demand quick wins, making it difficult for leaders to maintain focus on long-term objectives.

Great leaders navigate these challenges by clearly communicating their long-term vision and demonstrating the value of patience and persistence. They understand that while short-term results are important, they should not dictate strategy at the expense of future growth. Leaders with a long-term perspective often engage in transparent, open dialogue with stakeholders to explain why certain decisions, though not immediately profitable, are necessary for sustainable success. They balance the need for short-term performance with the pursuit of long-term goals, creating a leadership strategy that is both responsive and visionary.

At its core, the difference between short-term results and long-term impact comes down to the depth and breadth of a leader's vision. Great leaders think beyond immediate gains, focusing on how their actions today will shape the future of their organizations and the world. They are not satisfied with quick wins or superficial achievements; instead, they seek to create enduring value that benefits their organizations, their people, and society as a whole.

Leaders who prioritize long-term impact build legacies that outlast their tenure. They invest in people, innovation, and sustainability, ensuring that the foundations they lay today will continue to support success for years to come. By focusing on long-term impact, great leaders do more than just lead—they transform, leaving behind organizations and systems that are stronger, more resilient, and more capable of thriving in the future.

In leadership, endurance is not just an admirable quality but a fundamental requirement. True leadership demands a deep commitment to guiding people, organizations, and initiatives through adversity, uncertainty, and complex changes. Enduring leaders possess the resilience to face setbacks, the patience to await long-term results, and the adaptability to adjust course as circumstances evolve. In today's rapidly changing world, the leaders who rise above the rest are those who understand the importance of endurance in navigating the complexities of business and societal change.

As the business environment becomes increasingly interconnected and dynamic, the pressure on leaders is immense. Leaders must be prepared to adapt to technological innovations, global competition, fluctuating economic conditions, and shifts in social values. They must inspire trust and confidence even as they grapple with uncertainty and setbacks. This is where the qualities of resilience and patience prove to be invaluable. By cultivating these traits, leaders can foster a mindset that embraces the challenges of long-term leadership while staying grounded in their values and mission.

Endurance is not just about survival—it is about thriving in the face of adversity. It is the ability to keep moving forward when the path is unclear, to maintain focus on long-term goals even when progress seems slow, and to lead others through uncertainty with clarity and conviction. Endurance is what enables leaders to balance the demands of today with the promise of tomorrow, ensuring that they—and their organizations—can sustain success over the long haul.

Resilience is the core attribute that allows leaders to recover from setbacks and maintain their commitment to long-term goals. Without resilience, the inevitable challenges and difficulties that arise in leadership would become insurmountable. Resilient leaders are able to face adversity head-on, turning obstacles into opportunities for growth. They view challenges not as threats but as chances to innovate, adapt, and strengthen their leadership.

One leader who has exemplified resilience over the decades is Warren Buffett, the legendary investor and CEO of Berkshire Hathaway. Buffett's career has been marked by his ability to stay the course during periods of market volatility, economic downturns, and external pressures. Throughout his long and successful career, Buffett has navigated recessions, financial crises, and the dot-com bubble with a steady hand and unwavering belief in his investment philosophy. His resilience is rooted in a long-term approach, refusing to be swayed by short-term market fluctuations or trends.

Buffett's resilience is also evident in his willingness to learn from failure and remain patient during tough times. He has always emphasized the importance of investing in companies with strong fundamentals rather than chasing quick gains or following market fads. This approach has not only allowed him to recover from setbacks but has also built one of the most successful investment portfolios in history. His resilience, combined with his patience and commitment to long-term thinking, has made him a model of enduring leadership in the business world.

Leaders like Buffett demonstrate that resilience is not about avoiding failure—it is about how one responds to failure. Great leaders know that setbacks are inevitable, but they also understand that these challenges provide valuable opportunities for reflection, learning, and growth. Resilience allows leaders to persevere, even when the road ahead is difficult, and to emerge stronger on the other side.

To build resilience, leaders must be willing to embrace failure as a learning experience rather than a personal or organizational defeat. This means cultivating a mindset that views mistakes and challenges as opportunities for growth rather than signs of weakness. Leaders who foster resilience in themselves are better equipped to guide their organizations through turbulent times, ensuring that they remain focused on their long-term vision.

Resilience also requires a deep sense of emotional intelligence. Leaders who are in tune with their emotions, as well as the emotions of their teams, are better able to manage stress and remain calm under pressure. Emotional intelligence allows leaders to build strong relationships, foster trust, and create a supportive environment where people can thrive, even during difficult times.

In a culture that often celebrates speed, efficiency, and quick results, patience is a leadership quality that is frequently overlooked. Yet, for leaders who are committed to creating lasting impact, patience is an essential trait. Enduring leaders understand that meaningful change and sustainable success do not happen overnight. They recognize that complex problems require long-term solutions, and they are willing to invest time and energy into building a solid foundation for future growth.

Warren Buffett, once again, exemplifies the power of patience in leadership. Known for his long-term investment strategy, Buffett has often said that his favorite holding period for a stock is "forever." His approach to investing is based on the belief that true value is created over time and that patience is the key to unlocking that value. This philosophy has enabled Buffett to avoid the pitfalls of short-termism, focusing instead on the underlying strength of the businesses he invests in, even when short-term market conditions are unfavorable.

Buffett's patience is evident not only in his investment strategy but also in his leadership of Berkshire Hathaway. Over the years, he has built a conglomerate that is known for its stability, long-term growth, and ethical business practices. Rather than seeking quick wins or short-term profits, Buffett has consistently emphasized the importance of building companies with strong fundamentals that can weather the ups and downs of the market. His leadership exemplifies the idea that patience is not about waiting passively—it is about making thoughtful, deliberate decisions that will pay off in the long run.

Leaders who prioritize patience are better able to navigate the complexities of leadership because they understand that progress often comes in increments rather than leaps. They are not easily discouraged by slow progress or setbacks and have the foresight to see how today's decisions will shape the future. Patience allows leaders to stay committed to their vision, even when results are not immediately visible.

Cultivating patience as a leader requires a long-term mindset. Leaders must focus on their broader goals and remain committed to their mission, even when immediate results are not forthcoming. They must resist the pressure to prioritize short-term gains over long-term sustainability, recognizing that lasting success requires steady, consistent effort.

Patience also requires the ability to trust in the process. Leaders who are patient understand that meaningful change takes time and that progress often involves overcoming challenges and setbacks. By maintaining a sense of calm and perspective, they can inspire their teams to stay focused on their goals and continue working toward their vision, even when the path ahead is uncertain.

In today's world, where complexity is the norm rather than the exception, endurance is critical for leaders who want to navigate change and uncertainty effectively. Leaders are constantly faced with competing demands, shifting market conditions, and evolving societal expectations. Endurance provides the fortitude to continue pushing forward, even when the future is unclear.

Enduring leaders possess adaptability, which allows them to pivot when necessary while maintaining their commitment to their long-term goals. Rather than being rigid in their approach, they are flexible and open to new ideas, adjusting their strategies as circumstances change. This adaptability ensures that they can continue moving forward, even when the path to success is not straightforward.

At the same time, enduring leaders are skilled at making decisions in uncertain environments. They understand that complexity often means there is no single "right" answer, and they are comfortable making thoughtful, informed decisions even when the outcome is uncertain. By gathering diverse perspectives, analyzing risks, and learning from past experiences, they can make decisions that keep their organizations moving toward their long-term vision.

Collaboration is another key component of enduring leadership. Leaders who recognize that they cannot do it all alone build strong, resilient teams and foster a culture of shared responsibility. They delegate tasks effectively and trust their teams to contribute to the organization's success. This collaborative approach ensures that the organization can adapt to challenges and continue thriving, even in the face of complexity.

While resilience and patience are critical for individual leaders, they are equally important for the teams and organizations they lead. Great leaders understand that building a resilient, patient organization requires fostering these qualities in others. A resilient team is one that can adapt to change, learn from failure, and stay motivated during difficult times. A patient team is one that understands the value of long-term goals and is willing to invest in the process of achieving them.

Leaders can cultivate resilience and patience in their teams by creating a culture of continuous learning and improvement. This involves encouraging experimentation, celebrating successes, and viewing failures as opportunities for growth. When teams feel supported in their efforts to learn and improve, they become more adaptable and resilient in the face of change.

Transparency and trust are also essential for building resilience and patience in teams. Leaders who are open about the challenges and opportunities the organization faces create an environment where team members feel empowered to contribute to solutions. By fostering a sense of trust and collaboration, leaders can build teams that are capable of enduring difficult times while staying focused on their long-term goals.

Essentially, endurance is one of the most powerful qualities a leader can possess. In a world of constant change and complexity, the ability to remain resilient and patient is what distinguishes great leaders from the rest. Enduring leaders understand that success is not achieved overnight but through sustained effort, learning, and adaptability. They are willing to take the long view, investing in their people, their organizations, and their values in a way that creates lasting, positive impact.

By fostering resilience and patience in themselves and their teams, leaders can navigate the complexities of business and societal change with confidence and clarity. They become not just leaders of today but stewards of the future, leaving behind a legacy of strength, adaptability, and sustained success. In the end, it is the leaders who endure—those who persist through adversity, remain committed to their long-term vision and inspire others to do the same—who create the most meaningful and lasting change.

Resilience is the backbone of enduring leadership. It allows leaders and their teams to recover from setbacks, maintain focus on long-term objectives, and persevere through adversity. The following tools provide a structured approach to developing resilience, helping leaders cultivate this essential trait both within themselves and across their organizations.

Tool 1. The Personal Resilience Reflection Tool

Before leaders can foster resilience in their teams, they must first build it within themselves. The Personal Resilience Reflection Tool is designed to help leaders assess their current levels of resilience, identify areas for improvement, and develop strategies for managing stress and overcoming challenges. This tool encourages deep reflection on how you react to adversity and how you can strengthen your ability to bounce back.

Steps to Use the Personal Resilience Reflection Tool:

- **Self-Assessment**: Begin by reflecting on a recent challenge or setback you have experienced in your leadership role. How did you respond emotionally and mentally? Did you feel overwhelmed, or were you able to stay focused on solutions? How quickly were you able to regain your footing and continue moving forward?

- **Identify Coping Mechanisms**: List your coping mechanisms or strategies to manage stress during this challenge. Were they effective? Did you rely on external support, such as mentors or peers, or did you handle it alone? Consider whether your strategies for managing stress and uncertainty need adjustment.

- **Set Goals for Improvement**: Based on your reflection, identify areas where you would like to improve your resilience. Do you need to develop better stress-management techniques? Would you benefit from seeking support more frequently or developing a stronger work-life balance? Set concrete goals for how you will improve your resilience in future challenges.

- **Develop a Resilience Action Plan**: Create a personal action plan that outlines specific steps you can take to build your resilience. This might include adopting mindfulness practices, setting boundaries to avoid burnout, or engaging in regular self-care activities that help you maintain your emotional and mental well-being.

This tool helps leaders strengthen their ability to recover from setbacks and maintain their focus on long-term goals, no matter the challenges they face.

Tool 2. The Team Resilience Building Workshop

To cultivate resilience within your team, leaders can conduct a resilience-building workshop. This workshop encourages open dialogue, collective problem-solving, and the development of a team-wide strategy for dealing with future challenges. It fosters a culture of support, trust, and adaptability, ensuring that your team can stay resilient in the face of uncertainty.

Steps to Facilitate a Team Resilience Building Workshop:

- **Opening Discussion**: Begin the workshop by discussing the concept of resilience. What does resilience mean to the team? Encourage team members to share their personal experiences of overcoming challenges and how they managed to stay focused on their goals during difficult times.

- **Identify Team Strengths and Weaknesses**: As a group, brainstorm the strengths your team already has that contribute to resilience. This might include strong communication, mutual support, or adaptability. Then, identify areas where the team could improve. Are there processes that break down under pressure? Does the team struggle with motivation after setbacks?

- **Problem-Solving Scenarios**: Present the team with hypothetical scenarios involving significant challenges—such as a sudden market downturn, a major project delay, or losing a key team member. As a team, work through these scenarios to identify how you would handle the situation, what strategies you would use to maintain focus, and how you would adapt to the new reality.

- **Create a Team Resilience Plan**: Based on the discussion, create a resilience plan for the team. This plan should outline strategies for maintaining open communication, supporting each other through stress, and adapting to unexpected challenges. Assign roles to ensure that different team members are responsible for fostering resilience in specific areas, such as morale, problem-solving, and workload management.

The Team Resilience Building Workshop creates a shared sense of purpose and ensures that everyone is equipped with the mindset and tools to handle future challenges as a united front.

Exercise 1. The Future-Proofing Exercise

One of the key aspects of long-term planning is preparing for the unknown. The Future-Proofing Exercise helps leaders and their teams anticipate potential challenges and risks that could impact the organization in the future while also identifying opportunities for growth and innovation.

Steps for Conducting the Future-Proofing Exercise:

- **Identify Key Trends and Risks**: Begin by brainstorming potential trends, risks, and disruptions that could affect your organization over the next five to ten years. This could include technological advancements, economic changes, regulatory shifts, or societal trends. Encourage team members to think broadly and consider both internal and external factors.

- **Prioritize Challenges**: Once you have identified potential risks, prioritize them based on their likelihood and potential impact on your organization. Which risks are most critical to address in your long-term planning? Which are more uncertain but still worth considering?

- **Develop Contingency Plans**: For each prioritized challenge, develop a contingency plan. How will the organization respond if this challenge becomes a reality? What actions can be taken now to mitigate the risk? Consider building flexibility into your long-term strategy so that you can adapt to new challenges as they arise.

- **Identify Opportunities for Innovation**: In addition to focusing on risks, use this exercise to identify potential opportunities for innovation and growth. Are there trends that could create new markets or products for your organization? Are there areas where you can differentiate from competitors by adapting faster to change?

By thinking proactively about the future and developing contingency plans, leaders ensure that their long-term strategy is resilient and capable of adapting to whatever the future may bring.

Exercise 2. The Resilient Roadmap Planning Tool

The Resilient Roadmap Planning Tool helps leaders map out their long-term goals while incorporating resilience-building strategies at each stage of the journey. This tool ensures that the roadmap to success is not rigid but adaptable to changes and challenges that arise along the way.

Steps for Using the Resilient Roadmap Planning Tool:

- **Define Long-Term Objectives**: Start by clearly defining your long-term goals for the organization. These could be financial targets, cultural transformations, market expansions, or sustainability initiatives. Be specific about what success looks like for your organization five, ten, or even twenty years down the line.

- **Identify Milestones**: Break down your long-term objectives into smaller, achievable milestones. These milestones should serve as checkpoints along the way to measure progress. Ensure that these milestones are realistic but also challenging enough to keep the organization moving forward.

- **Incorporate Resilience Strategies**: At each milestone, identify strategies that will help build resilience within the organization. These might include fostering a culture of continuous learning, creating space for innovation and adaptability, or developing leadership skills across the team. Think about how each stage of your roadmap can strengthen your team's ability to handle future challenges.

- **Monitor and Adapt**: The Resilient Roadmap is a living document. Build in regular review periods where you and your team reassess the roadmap's progress and relevance. As new challenges or opportunities arise, be prepared to adjust your milestones and strategies to reflect the current landscape. Adaptability is key to ensuring that the long-term plan remains relevant and achievable.

The Resilient Roadmap Planning Tool allows leaders to take a structured approach to long-term planning while remaining flexible and adaptable to changes in the environment.

Chapter 7
Activating Infinite Potential in Others

Leadership, at its core, is not merely about the personal growth or success of the leader. In its most profound sense, leadership is about fostering the growth of others, unlocking the potential that lies within each individual, and creating an environment where those around the leader can thrive. The most effective leaders understand that their true legacy is not defined by their own accomplishments, but by the impact they have on the people they lead, shaping a culture that encourages development, collaboration, and shared success.

To lead well is to recognize that your influence extends far beyond your own growth. It means cultivating a space where others feel empowered to discover and harness their strengths, a space where innovation is encouraged, and where individuals are motivated to reach for goals that may have once seemed unattainable. Great leaders are, in essence, catalysts—through their guidance, they ignite potential and create a ripple effect of growth, learning, and achievement within their organizations.

When a leader's focus is solely on personal achievement, their impact is inevitably limited. They may find short-term success, but they will struggle to sustain it or to inspire long-term growth within the organization. In contrast, leaders who commit to unlocking the potential in those around them create a multiplier effect. By nurturing talent, fostering innovation, and investing in the development of their teams, these leaders build a legacy that extends far beyond their own tenure. Their organizations become stronger, more adaptable, and more resilient.

Effective leadership involves a fundamental shift in mindset: from self-centred achievement to empowering others to succeed. Leaders who embrace this responsibility understand that their own success is intrinsically tied to the growth of those they lead. They prioritize the development of their team members, creating opportunities for them to learn, grow, and take on new challenges. This is not merely an act of delegation but an intentional effort to elevate others, nurture their potential, and create a culture where everyone feels empowered to contribute their best.

Take, for example, Indra Nooyi, the former CEO of PepsiCo, who embodied this principle in her leadership. Nooyi was known for her belief that leadership was about serving others and helping them grow into their full potential. She prioritised mentoring and developing her employees, providing them with the support and guidance they needed to rise into leadership roles. For Nooyi, success was not measured by individual accolades but by the collective success of the people around her. She understood that by empowering others, she was ensuring the long-term success of the organization.

This responsibility to empower others extends beyond professional development; it includes helping individuals find a sense of purpose in their work. Great leaders tap into the motivations and strengths of each person they lead, creating an environment where individuals feel seen, valued, and capable of achieving great things. By focusing on unlocking the potential within their teams, leaders create a more engaged, productive, and innovative organization.

One of the most effective ways to unlock potential in others is through mentorship and coaching. Both practices involve investing time and energy into helping individuals grow, but they do so in slightly different ways. Mentorship often involves sharing personal experiences, offering guidance, and providing support as individuals navigate their careers. It is about helping others see their potential and showing them the path to realizing it. Coaching, on the other hand, is more about facilitating self-discovery—helping individuals find their own solutions to challenges, encouraging critical thinking, and fostering a sense of ownership over their growth.

Mentorship and coaching are not passive endeavors. They require active listening, thoughtful questioning, and a genuine commitment to the development of the person being mentored or coached. Leaders who embrace these roles help others identify their strengths, recognize their areas for growth, and build the confidence to take on new challenges. Effective mentors and coaches know that their job is not to provide all the answers but to guide individuals toward discovering their own path to success.

This makes mentorship and coaching so powerful—they empower individuals to take control of their own development. Leaders who invest in the growth of their people through mentorship and coaching create a culture of continuous learning where individuals feel supported but also challenged to grow. They understand that unlocking potential is not a one-size-fits-all process. Each person has unique talents, motivations, and challenges, and it is the leader's responsibility to tailor their approach to meet the needs of each individual.

When leaders focus on unlocking the potential of those around them, they create a ripple effect that extends far beyond their immediate circle of influence. This is known as the "multiplier effect"—the idea that when leaders empower individuals to contribute their best, they multiply their impact across the organization. Empowered individuals are more engaged, more innovative, and more willing to take ownership of their work, which in turn leads to higher levels of performance and collective achievement.

Leaders who embrace this mindset understand that their own success is amplified by the success of their teams. They are not focused on accumulating personal accolades or power; instead, they take pride in seeing others excel. Their legacy is not defined by individual accomplishments, but by the growth and development they have fostered in those around them.

Leaders who unlock potential in others strengthen the overall resilience and adaptability of the organization. When individuals feel empowered to take ownership of their work and contribute their ideas, the organization becomes more agile, able to innovate and respond to change more effectively. This shared sense of ownership and contribution creates a culture of continuous improvement, where each person is invested in the organisation's collective success.

Consider how Nelson Mandela approached leadership. His success as a leader was not solely based on his own personal achievements but on his ability to empower others to take ownership of the movement for justice and equality. Mandela understood that unlocking the potential of others—whether it was the people of South Africa or the global community—was the key to lasting change. His leadership was defined by his ability to inspire, elevate, and empower those around him to believe in their capacity to make a difference.

Unlocking potential in others requires creating a culture where development and empowerment are prioritized. Leaders must foster an environment where individuals feel safe to take risks, explore new ideas, and learn from their mistakes. This involves setting clear expectations, providing growth opportunities, and offering ongoing feedback and support.

A culture of development is built on trust. Leaders must trust their teams to take ownership of their work, and team members must trust that their leaders have their best interests at heart. This trust is cultivated through transparency, open communication, and a genuine commitment to the growth of each individual. Leaders who create this type of culture encourage innovation, creativity, and a willingness to take on new challenges—knowing that even if mistakes are made, they are part of the learning process.

At the same time, leaders must ensure that individuals have the resources and support they need to succeed. This might include providing access to training programs, offering opportunities for cross-functional projects, or facilitating mentorship and coaching relationships. Leaders who invest in the development of their people create a pipeline of talent that not only benefits the individuals but also strengthens the organization as a whole.

Leaders must recognize and celebrate the successes of their teams. By acknowledging both individual and collective achievements, leaders reinforce the value of development and growth, creating a positive feedback loop that encourages further progress. This culture of recognition fosters a sense of pride and ownership in the work being done, further unlocking the potential of those involved.

At its highest level, leadership is not about personal glory or individual achievement—it is about serving others. The most effective leaders understand that their primary responsibility is to unlock the potential of those around them, creating an environment where individuals feel empowered to grow, innovate, and contribute their best. This mindset shifts leadership from a self-centred pursuit to one that is grounded in empowerment, collaboration, and collective success.

Unlocking potential in others requires intention, investment, and a genuine commitment to the development of those you lead. Leaders who embrace this responsibility multiply their impact, creating a culture of growth and innovation that drives long-term success. By fostering the growth of others, these leaders create organizations that are resilient, adaptable, and capable of thriving in an ever-changing world. Ultimately, the true measure of a leader's success is not what they accomplish alone but the legacy of growth, empowerment, and potential they leave behind.

Empowerment is one of the most powerful tools in a leader's arsenal. It is the ability to foster an environment where individuals feel inspired, capable, and supported to exceed their own expectations and limitations. Empowering leadership creates a culture of trust, collaboration, and growth, where people are not only encouraged to take ownership of their work but are also given the tools, resources, and confidence they need to achieve their fullest potential. The most effective leaders understand that their success is tied directly to their ability to lift others, creating an atmosphere where each person believes in their capacity to contribute something meaningful and, ultimately, to exceed what they once thought was possible.

The essence of empowerment lies in trust and autonomy. Leaders who empower others do not micromanage; instead, they provide clear direction and expectations while giving their teams the freedom to innovate, make decisions, and take ownership of their work. By cultivating an environment where individuals are encouraged to explore their own potential, leaders unlock the latent abilities and creativity within their teams, enabling them to accomplish far more than they would in a more restrictive or hierarchical structure.

But, empowerment is not simply about delegation or allowing autonomy. It requires a proactive approach that nurtures growth, provides support, and builds confidence in individuals. Empowerment is about creating the conditions in which people feel motivated to take on challenges and stretch themselves beyond their perceived limits, knowing they have the support and resources to succeed.

Empowering leadership is about striking the right balance between guidance and freedom. Leaders who excel at empowerment are skilled at providing the structure and clarity that people need to understand the goals and values of the organization while also encouraging autonomy and innovation in how those goals are achieved. The leader's role is not to dictate each step but to create an environment where individuals feel safe to take initiative, experiment, and bring their own ideas to the table.

Consider the leadership style of Richard Branson, founder of the Virgin Group, who is known for empowering his teams to take ownership and make decisions. Branson has famously said, "Train people well enough so they can leave, treat them well enough so they don't want to." His leadership approach is rooted in the belief that people thrive when they are trusted to take charge, make decisions, and even learn from their mistakes. Branson fosters a culture where employees feel supported and valued, which in turn inspires loyalty, innovation, and a sense of ownership over their work. By giving his teams the freedom to innovate, Branson has been able to lead a diverse and highly successful global enterprise.

Leaders who empower others see their role as facilitators of success. They recognize that their job is to provide the vision, resources, and support necessary for individuals to thrive. They also understand that empowerment requires an ongoing investment in the growth and development of their people. This involves creating opportunities for learning, offering constructive feedback, and ensuring that individuals have the tools they need to succeed.

At the heart of empowerment is trust. Leaders must trust their teams to take ownership of their work, make decisions, and solve problems in ways that align with the organization's goals. In turn, individuals must trust that their leaders will provide them with the support, resources, and guidance they need to succeed without undermining their autonomy. Trust is the foundation upon which a culture of empowerment is built.

Building trust starts with clear communication. Leaders who empower others are transparent about expectations, goals, and the broader vision of the organization. They ensure that their teams have a deep understanding of what is expected of them, while also giving them the freedom to determine how they will achieve those objectives. When individuals have clarity about the end goal but are trusted to choose their path to get there, they feel more engaged, motivated, and invested in the outcome.

A culture of trust also requires leaders to embrace a certain level of risk. Empowering others means allowing them to take risks, try new approaches, and even make mistakes. Leaders who are too focused on controlling outcomes or avoiding failure stifle innovation and prevent their teams from realizing their full potential. Instead, empowering leaders create a safe environment where failure is seen as a valuable learning experience. They encourage individuals to take calculated risks and support them when things do not go as planned, using setbacks as opportunities for growth.

Empowerment goes hand in hand with personal and professional growth. Leaders who are committed to empowering their teams recognize that continuous development is essential for unlocking potential. By investing in the growth of their people, they ensure that individuals have the skills, knowledge, and confidence to take on new challenges and excel in their roles.

One way to encourage growth is by creating opportunities for learning and development. This could include formal training programs, mentorship opportunities, or cross-functional projects that allow individuals to expand their skill sets and gain new experiences. Leaders who prioritize development understand that empowerment is not about leaving people to figure things out on their own but about providing them with the resources and support they need to grow.

Mentorship is a particularly powerful tool for empowerment. Leaders who take on the role of mentor provide guidance, share their experiences, and help individuals navigate challenges. A good mentor helps others see their potential and offers encouragement as they push beyond their comfort zones. By actively supporting the development of their people, leaders not only empower individuals but also create a culture of continuous improvement.

Oprah Winfrey is an example of a leader who has empowered others through personal growth and development. Throughout her career, Winfrey has championed the idea that personal empowerment comes from self-awareness, education, and a commitment to lifelong learning. She has used her platform to inspire millions to overcome adversity and achieve their goals. As a leader, Winfrey has fostered environments where those around her feel encouraged to pursue their dreams and develop their talents, whether it is through her work in media, philanthropy, or mentoring young women.

Empowerment requires more than just encouragement—it requires action. Leaders must ensure that their teams have the resources, tools, and support necessary to achieve their goals. Without adequate support, individuals may feel overwhelmed or incapable of delivering their best work, undermining empowerment's very purpose.

Providing support involves offering guidance and feedback when needed while giving individuals the space to make decisions and solve problems independently. Empowering leaders strike a balance between offering support and fostering autonomy, ensuring that individuals feel both capable and confident in their abilities. This support might include access to technology, training, or even emotional support during challenging times.

Effective feedback is another crucial element of empowerment. Leaders who empower others provide constructive, actionable feedback and focus on growth. They help individuals recognize their strengths and areas for improvement, guiding them toward solutions without diminishing their sense of ownership. By providing thoughtful feedback, leaders help individuals build confidence and resilience, enabling them to take on even greater challenges in the future.

One of the most profound effects of empowering leadership is the confidence it instils in individuals. When people feel empowered, they begin to see themselves as capable of achieving more than they previously thought possible. They are more likely to take initiative, bring new ideas to the table, and step into leadership roles themselves.

Empowering leaders actively work to build this confidence by recognizing and celebrating successes, no matter how small. By acknowledging progress and achievements, leaders reinforce a sense of accomplishment and capability in their teams. This positive reinforcement encourages individuals to keep pushing themselves, to take on new challenges, and to strive for even greater achievements.

Encouraging risk-taking is another important aspect of building confidence. Empowering leaders creates an environment where individuals feel comfortable stepping outside their comfort zones and experimenting with new ideas. They foster a culture of curiosity and innovation, where failure is not seen as something to be avoided but as an integral part of the learning process. By creating a safe space for risk-taking, leaders encourage individuals to pursue bold ideas and take ownership of their successes and failures alike.

Empowering leadership is about creating an environment where individuals feel inspired, capable, and supported to achieve more than they believe possible. By fostering trust, autonomy, and personal growth, leaders unlock the potential within their teams, enabling them to contribute their best ideas, take ownership of their work, and push beyond their limits. Empowerment is not just about delegation—it is about providing the resources, guidance, and support needed to help others grow into their full potential.

Leaders who embrace empowerment understand that their role is not to control or dictate but to facilitate and enable. They recognize that lifting others creates a ripple effect of growth, innovation, and success that benefits the entire organization. Ultimately, empowering leadership creates a culture of continuous development, where individuals feel motivated to strive for excellence, take on new challenges, and achieve more than they ever thought possible. Empowering others is not just an act of leadership—it is an act of service and the key to unlocking greatness in individuals and organizations.

Tool 1. Mentorship Techniques for Leadership Development

Mentorship is one of the most powerful tools for developing leadership. Effective mentorship provides individuals with the guidance, support, and confidence needed to step into leadership roles. The goal of mentorship is not simply to impart knowledge but to help individuals recognize their own potential, build their leadership skills, and navigate challenges.

The Mentorship Framework

To ensure that mentorship is effective, leaders can use a structured framework that provides clear goals, regular check-ins, and continuous feedback. This framework helps mentors provide the right balance of support and challenge, encouraging mentees to grow while allowing them the space to take ownership of their development.

Steps for Using the Mentorship Framework:

- **Set Clear Objectives**: At the beginning of the mentorship relationship, it is important to establish clear objectives. What does the mentee hope to achieve through mentorship? These objectives could include improving specific leadership skills, preparing for a leadership role, or developing a broader understanding of the organization's strategic goals.

- **Create a Growth Plan**: Once objectives are established, the mentor and mentee should work together to create a personalized growth plan. This plan should outline the skills and experiences the mentee needs to develop and specific actions they will take to achieve their goals. For example, if the mentee wants to improve their communication skills, the plan might include opportunities to present at meetings or lead team discussions.

- **Regular Check-Ins**: Mentorship requires ongoing dialogue and reflection. Regular check-ins provide an opportunity to assess progress, address challenges, and adjust the growth plan as needed. During these check-ins, mentors should ask open-ended questions that encourage self-reflection, such as "What challenges have you encountered, and how did you handle them?" or "What leadership skills have you noticed improving?"

- **Provide Constructive Feedback**: Feedback is essential for growth. Mentors should offer constructive feedback that helps the mentee recognize both their strengths and areas for improvement. Effective feedback is specific, actionable, and delivered in a way that encourages the mentee to continue developing their skills.

Reverse Mentorship

A valuable technique in leadership development is reverse mentorship, where younger or less experienced employees mentor senior leaders. This practice not only benefits the mentor by giving them the opportunity to share their expertise and perspective but also helps senior leaders stay connected to emerging trends, technologies, and ideas. Reverse mentorship fosters a two-way learning relationship that empowers both parties and creates a culture of knowledge-sharing and collaboration.

Steps to Implement Reverse Mentorship:

- Pair junior employees with senior leaders based on complementary skills or shared goals.

- Set clear expectations for the mentorship relationship, emphasizing that the junior mentor offers valuable insights.

- Encourage open dialogue, where both the mentor and mentee feel comfortable asking questions and sharing knowledge.

Tool 2. Creating Leadership Opportunities

Leadership cannot be learned in a vacuum. To develop leadership skills, individuals must be given opportunities to lead. Creating these opportunities requires leaders to intentionally delegate tasks, encourage initiative, and give individuals the space to take ownership of projects or decisions. These leadership opportunities should be designed to challenge individuals while providing them with the support and resources they need to succeed.

The Delegation of Authority Model

One effective way to create leadership opportunities is through the delegation of authority. This model involves assigning responsibility for key decisions or projects to individuals, allowing them to step into a leadership role. By delegating meaningful tasks, leaders empower individuals to develop their problem-solving, decision-making, and leadership skills in real-world scenarios.

Steps to Implement the Delegation of Authority Model:

- **Identify Leadership Potential**: Identify individuals who demonstrate leadership potential or are willing to take on new challenges. These individuals might not yet have formal leadership roles, but they show initiative, creativity, or a desire for growth.

- **Delegate Meaningful Projects**: Choose projects or decisions that are significant enough to challenge the individual but within their capability to manage. This might involve leading a cross-functional team, managing a new initiative, or making strategic decisions in a specific area.

- **Provide Support and Guidance**: While the individual takes ownership of the project or decision, the leader should remain available to provide support and guidance as needed. This support might include regular check-ins, feedback sessions, or resources that help the individual succeed.

- **Allow for Autonomy**: Empowerment is key to this model. While leaders should provide support, allowing individuals the autonomy to make decisions and learn from their experiences is important. Trusting individuals to take ownership of their work builds confidence and fosters leadership growth.

Rotational Leadership Programs

Another way to create leadership opportunities is through rotational leadership programs, where individuals rotate through different departments or teams, gaining exposure to various aspects of the organization. This cross-functional experience allows them to develop a broader understanding of the business, build relationships across teams, and practice leadership in different contexts.

Steps to Create a Rotational Leadership Program:

- **Design the Program**: Structure the program to include rotations in key areas of the organization, such as operations, finance, marketing, and strategy. Each rotation should provide the individual with leadership opportunities, such as managing a project or leading a team in that department.

- **Set Learning Objectives**: For each rotation, set specific learning objectives that align with the individual's leadership development goals. These might include developing strategic thinking, improving communication skills, or learning how to manage resources effectively.

- **Debrief After Each Rotation**: After each rotation, debrief with the individual to discuss what they learned, how they applied leadership skills in that context, and what challenges they encountered. This reflection helps solidify the learning experience and prepares them for the next rotation.

Tool 3. Fostering Innovation to Develop Leadership

Innovation is a critical component of leadership development. Leaders must be able to think creatively, solve complex problems, and navigate uncertainty. By fostering a culture of innovation, leaders can encourage individuals to develop these critical leadership skills. Innovation requires the freedom to explore new ideas and the support to experiment, take risks, and learn from failure.

Innovation Labs

One way to foster innovation and develop leadership is through the creation of innovation labs. These labs provide a structured environment where individuals or teams can experiment with new ideas, test prototypes, and explore creative solutions to challenges facing the organization. Innovation labs encourage individuals to think like leaders by giving them ownership of projects and the freedom to explore new approaches.

Steps to Create an Innovation Lab:

- **Define the Scope**: Identify the challenges or opportunities the innovation lab will focus on. This could range from improving operational efficiency to developing new products or services. Ensure that the scope is broad enough to encourage creativity but focused enough to drive tangible results.

- **Form Cross-Functional Teams**: Bring together individuals from different departments or areas of expertise to collaborate on innovation projects. Cross-functional teams foster diverse perspectives and encourage creative problem-solving.

- **Encourage Experimentation**: In the innovation lab, emphasize the importance of experimentation. Encourage teams to test new ideas, iterate on solutions, and learn from both successes and failures. The goal is to innovate and develop leadership skills such as critical thinking, collaboration, and risk management.

- **Provide Leadership Opportunities**: Assign leadership roles within the lab, such as project leads or innovation champions. These roles allow individuals to practice leadership in a dynamic, fast-paced environment where adaptability and creativity are essential.

Innovation Challenges

An innovation challenge is another effective way to foster leadership development through creative problem-solving. In an innovation challenge, individuals or teams are tasked with addressing a specific organizational challenge or opportunity with the goal of developing innovative solutions.

Steps to Implement an Innovation Challenge:

- **Present the Challenge**: Identify a pressing challenge facing the organization, such as improving customer satisfaction or reducing costs. Present this challenge to individuals or teams, encouraging them to propose creative solutions.

- **Set Parameters**: Provide guidelines for the innovation challenge, such as a timeline for developing and presenting solutions. While it is important to set parameters, ensure that teams have enough flexibility to explore a range of ideas.

- **Facilitate the Process**: Support the teams throughout the challenge by providing access to resources, tools, and mentors. While individuals should take ownership of their ideas, leaders should remain available to offer guidance and feedback.

- **Evaluate and Celebrate Solutions**: Once the challenge is complete, evaluate the proposed solutions based on criteria such as feasibility, creativity, and impact. Recognize and celebrate the most innovative ideas and consider implementing them within the organization. This recognition reinforces the importance of innovation and encourages continued leadership development.

Chapter 8
The Roadmap for Transformational Leadership

The Infinite Potential Leadership framework is not just a philosophy or an abstract theory. It is a set of guiding principles meant to be integrated into daily leadership practices—providing leaders with practical, actionable strategies to unlock growth in themselves and those around them. Leadership, especially in today's dynamic and ever-evolving environment, requires more than simply achieving short-term goals or managing day-to-day operations. It calls for a deep commitment to fostering an environment where continuous growth, adaptability, and innovation are central to both personal and organizational success.

Infinite Potential Leadership is the belief that both leaders and their teams have untapped capacities for transformation and improvement. The challenge is how to tap into this potential, especially when immediate pressures or external challenges often divert attention from the long-term vision. The key lies in making the principles of Infinite Potential Leadership part of your daily leadership approach—integrating them so naturally into your interactions and decision-making that they become the foundation of your leadership style.

One of the most fundamental aspects of Infinite Potential Leadership is cultivating a mindset of continuous growth, both for yourself as a leader and for those you lead. The idea is simple: every success, failure, and challenge provides an opportunity to learn, develop, and stretch beyond current capabilities. Leaders who adopt a growth-oriented mindset do not see setbacks as roadblocks but as valuable learning experiences that pave the way for future success. They foster this mindset not only within themselves but throughout their organization.

When applied to everyday leadership, this principle encourages leaders to create an environment where learning and development are part of the culture. It means establishing systems where team members feel safe to push boundaries, try new things, and learn from their mistakes. This environment is one where feedback is viewed as a tool for improvement, not criticism, and where efforts are rewarded, even if the results are not immediately perfect.

Imagine you are leading a team that has just launched a new product that did not meet expectations. Instead of focusing solely on the failure, a growth-oriented leader would gather the team to reflect on what was learned from the experience. They would encourage team members to share insights, explore what could be improved, and make adjustments to ensure future success. In doing so, the leader is focusing on results and reinforcing the idea that setbacks are part of the growth process. This shift in perspective builds a culture of resilience and adaptability, essential elements in any innovative organization.

By fostering this mindset within your team, you create an environment where individuals are motivated to continuously seek out opportunities for improvement, knowing that growth is valued as much as results. This approach drives innovation and empowers people to push beyond their perceived limits, unlocking new levels of potential.

Empowering others is central to the Infinite Potential Leadership framework. Leaders are not just responsible for their own growth—they have a duty to unlock the potential in those around them. Empowerment, however, is not about simply delegating tasks or allowing team members to operate independently. It involves creating the conditions in which individuals feel inspired, capable, and supported to stretch beyond their current abilities and achieve more than they thought possible.

The most effective leaders empower their teams by providing clear direction and vision but giving people the autonomy and trust to take ownership of their work. This requires a delicate balance: leaders must give their teams enough freedom to innovate and make decisions while still providing the support and guidance necessary to ensure success. When done correctly, this approach builds confidence and encourages creativity, driving both personal and organizational growth.

Take, for example, a leader in a rapidly changing industry. Instead of micromanaging every decision, they may choose to empower their team to adapt and respond to emerging challenges. This leader might provide the framework and vision for where the company needs to go but allow their team to develop strategies to get there. In this scenario, the team feels ownership over the process, which not only increases their engagement but also enhances their problem-solving abilities and fosters a culture of innovation.

Empowerment is about trust—trusting that people will rise to the challenge when given the opportunity and support to do so. It requires leaders to step back at times, allowing team members to make mistakes and learn from them while still offering the safety net of guidance when necessary. By empowering others, leaders create a ripple effect, multiplying their impact by enabling those around them to lead in their own right.

Infinite Potential Leadership thrives in an environment where innovation and adaptability are woven into the fabric of the organization. In today's world, where disruption and change are constants, leaders must foster a culture that encourages creativity and flexibility. This means moving away from rigid, hierarchical decision-making structures and creating spaces where new ideas are encouraged, risks are celebrated, and failures are seen as learning opportunities.

Innovation, by its very nature, involves stepping into the unknown. For this reason, leaders must create a safe space where team members feel comfortable taking risks without fear of judgment. This does not mean promoting reckless decision-making but rather encouraging calculated risks where individuals are given the freedom to experiment, test new ideas, and learn from the process. A leader who embraces innovation recognizes that not every idea will succeed, but the process of trying, learning, and iterating leads to breakthrough solutions.

Consider a company navigating the challenges of a saturated market. A leader focused on infinite potential might encourage cross-departmental teams to come together and brainstorm new ways to approach product development or service delivery. Instead of focusing solely on immediate profitability, this leader would emphasize the importance of exploring new ideas, even if they require an investment of time and resources. By fostering a culture of experimentation, the leader sets the stage for long-term success and adaptability in the face of changing market demands.

Adaptability is closely linked to innovation. Leaders who model adaptability show their teams that change is not something to be feared but embraced. They optimistically react to challenges, encouraging their teams to view obstacles as opportunities to grow and innovate. When faced with a shift in the market or a sudden disruption, these leaders pivot quickly, helping their teams stay focused on the broader goals while adapting to the new reality.

In a world full of uncertainties, resilience is a crucial element of successful leadership. Leaders who embody Infinite Potential Leadership understand that setbacks and challenges are inevitable. Rather than being derailed by obstacles, they use these moments as opportunities to build strength and resilience in themselves and their teams.

Resilience begins with mindset. Leaders who view setbacks as temporary and surmountable create a culture where challenges are seen as part of the growth process. Instead of blaming or reacting negatively to difficulties, they encourage reflection and learning. This approach not only helps individuals bounce back from setbacks more quickly but also strengthens the team's collective ability to handle adversity.

Imagine leading a team through a period of economic uncertainty. A resilient leader would not panic or overreact to short-term financial pressures. Instead, they would maintain a calm, solutions-oriented approach, confidently helping the team navigate the challenges and focus on long-term goals. By modeling resilience, this leader reassures the team that setbacks are a natural part of the journey and that success is still within reach, even if the path forward requires adjustments.

Resilience is also about support. Leaders need to create environments where people feel supported, especially during difficult times. This might mean providing emotional support, helping people manage stress, or simply offering words of encouragement. When individuals know they have the support of their leader, they are more likely to persevere and maintain their focus on long-term objectives.

Perhaps the most powerful way to apply the principles of Infinite Potential Leadership is by leading through example. Leaders set the tone for their teams; their actions speak louder than words. When leaders embody the values of growth, empowerment, innovation, and resilience in their own behavior, they naturally inspire those around them to do the same.

Leading by example means being intentional about how you show up as a leader every day. It means demonstrating a commitment to continuous learning by seeking out opportunities for personal growth and sharing your learning journey with your team. It means being transparent about the challenges you face as a leader and how you are working through them. It also means holding yourself accountable to the same standards you expect from others—whether that is in your work ethic, your openness to feedback, or your ability to navigate change with grace.

When leaders live the principles of Infinite Potential Leadership, they create an atmosphere of trust and authenticity. They show their teams that it is not only possible but expected to grow, adapt, and overcome obstacles. This kind of leadership is contagious—when people see their leaders pushing beyond their own limits, they feel inspired to do the same.

The principles of Infinite Potential Leadership are not reserved for extraordinary moments—they are meant to be woven into the fabric of everyday leadership. By fostering a growth-oriented mindset, empowering others, creating a culture of innovation, developing resilience, and leading by example, leaders can unlock the full potential in themselves and those around them.

Applying these principles daily helps leaders cultivate environments where individuals are inspired, capable, and supported to achieve more than they ever thought possible. It transforms leadership from a position of authority into a platform for empowerment and growth. In doing so, leaders who embrace Infinite Potential Leadership drive their own success and the success of their teams and organizations, creating a legacy of transformation that extends far beyond their immediate reach.

Leading transformational change is one of the most complex and demanding responsibilities of leadership. Unlike incremental improvements or routine problem-solving, transformational change seeks to fundamentally alter the way an organization operates, responds to challenges, and innovates for the future. It involves more than just adjusting processes or tweaking strategies—it is about creating a bold vision for the future, engaging stakeholders in a shared journey, and ensuring that the change is deeply integrated into the culture and fabric of the organization. To lead such change effectively, leaders must focus on three key pillars: visioning, stakeholder engagement, and communication strategies. These elements provide the framework necessary to navigate the complexities of change while inspiring and empowering teams to embrace the future.

Every successful transformation begins with a powerful vision. A clear, compelling vision serves as the guiding light for the organization, setting the direction and creating a sense of purpose that drives the change forward. Without a vision, teams can become lost in the day-to-day challenges of executing the change, and the transformation can lose momentum. A strong vision not only outlines the organisation's future state but also inspires people to believe in the possibility of that future. It provides a reason for change that goes beyond simply improving efficiency or increasing profitability—it connects to something larger, something aspirational.

Developing a transformational vision requires a deep understanding of the organisation's current state and the opportunities that lie ahead. It is about identifying where the organization needs to go, why it needs to change, and how this change will create long-term value. Leaders must ask themselves: What is the core challenge or opportunity driving this change? What will success look like when the transformation is complete? How will this change benefit not just the organization but all the stakeholders involved?

However, it is not enough to have a vision—the vision must be communicated effectively. It must be simple enough to be understood by everyone in the organization but bold enough to inspire excitement and action. Leaders should communicate the vision in a way that resonates emotionally with their teams, helping them see how their individual contributions are critical to achieving the larger goal. This emotional connection to the vision is what drives commitment and mobilizes people to take ownership of the change.

Moreover, the vision must align with the organization's core values. When the vision is deeply rooted in the values and culture of the organization, it becomes more than just a strategic initiative—it becomes a natural evolution of the organization's purpose and identity. This alignment helps to build trust and credibility, ensuring that employees, stakeholders, and partners see the transformation as a continuation of the organization's legacy rather than a radical departure from it.

Transformational change is not something that can be driven from the top down. For a transformation to be successful, it requires the active engagement and commitment of a wide range of stakeholders, both inside and outside the organization. These stakeholders may include employees, managers, executives, customers, investors, and even regulatory bodies, each of whom has a vested interest in the outcome of the change. Leaders must take a strategic approach to engaging these stakeholders, understanding their needs, motivations, and concerns, and working to build buy-in at every level.

The first step in engaging stakeholders is identifying who they are and understanding their unique perspectives on the change. Employees, for example, may be concerned about how the transformation will impact their roles or the security of their jobs, while investors may be focused on the long-term financial benefits of the change. On the other hand, customers may need reassurance that the transformation will enhance the products or services they rely on. By taking the time to understand these diverse viewpoints, leaders can tailor their messaging and engagement strategies to address each stakeholder group's specific concerns and interests.

One of the most effective ways to engage stakeholders is through collaboration and co-creation. Rather than presenting a fully formed plan for the transformation, leaders should involve stakeholders in the process of shaping the change. This might involve forming cross-functional teams to tackle specific aspects of the transformation, holding workshops to generate ideas and solutions, or soliciting feedback from customers and partners on how the change will impact them. When stakeholders are actively involved in designing the organisation's future state, they feel a sense of ownership over the change, making them more committed to its success.

For instance, in a large organization undergoing a digital transformation, leaders might form a steering committee composed of representatives from various departments—marketing, operations, IT, and finance—along with external partners and even customers. This committee would work together to identify the opportunities and challenges associated with the transformation, ensuring that diverse perspectives are incorporated into the planning process. By fostering collaboration across the organization, the leader builds a more robust and well-rounded transformation strategy and creates a network of advocates who will champion the change within their teams.

In addition to collaboration, leaders must be proactive in building relationships with key influencers and champions within the organization. These individuals, who hold formal or informal leadership roles, have the ability to sway the opinions of others and can play a critical role in driving the transformation forward. By engaging these influencers early and involving them in the planning and execution of the change, leaders can leverage their influence to build momentum and ensure that the transformation is embraced at every level of the organization.

Effective communication is the foundation of any successful transformational change effort. Without clear, consistent, and transparent communication, even the most well-conceived change initiatives can falter. Leaders must develop a communication strategy that informs stakeholders about the change, builds trust, manages expectations, and fosters a sense of shared purpose.

One of the most important aspects of communication during a transformation is helping people understand the "why" behind the change. It's not enough to explain what is happening—leaders must articulate why the change is necessary, how it aligns with the organization's broader mission, and what benefits it will bring. This context helps stakeholders connect emotionally with the transformation, seeing it not as a disruption but as an essential step toward a better future.

Suppose a company is implementing a significant restructuring to become more competitive. In that case, the leader must communicate not only the details of the restructuring but also why it is necessary to ensure the company's long-term survival and success. By framing the change in terms of the company's larger vision—such as becoming an industry leader in innovation—the leader helps employees understand the strategic importance of the transformation and how it will ultimately benefit everyone involved.

Once the rationale for the change has been communicated, leaders must focus on the "how." This means providing a clear roadmap for how the transformation will unfold, including key milestones, timelines, and the steps that will be taken to achieve the desired outcomes. This transparency is critical for building trust— when stakeholders know what to expect and how the change will impact them, they are more likely to feel confident and secure in their roles.

In addition to clarity, communication must be ongoing. Transformational change is not a one-time event but a process that unfolds over weeks, months, or even years. Throughout this process, leaders must provide regular updates on progress, address any challenges or roadblocks, and celebrate key wins along the way. This continuous flow of information helps to maintain momentum and ensures that stakeholders remain engaged and committed to the transformation.

Finally, leaders must recognize that communication is not just about delivering information but about creating dialogue. Stakeholders need to feel that their voices are heard and that their concerns are being addressed. Leaders should create opportunities for two-way communication, such as town halls, Q&A sessions, or focus groups, where stakeholders can ask questions, provide feedback, and share their perspectives. This type of open communication fosters a sense of inclusion and builds trust, ensuring that stakeholders feel like active participants in the change rather than passive recipients of decisions.

Leading transformational change is both an art and a science. It requires a bold vision that inspires and unites the organization, a strategic approach to stakeholder engagement that builds commitment and collaboration, and a communication strategy that fosters trust and transparency. By focusing on these three pillars—visioning, stakeholder engagement, and communication—leaders can guide their teams and organizations through the complexities of change, ensuring that the transformation is successful and sustainable.

The journey of transformational change is rarely straightforward. It is filled with challenges, setbacks, and moments of uncertainty. But with the right roadmap, leaders can navigate these obstacles and create a stronger, more resilient, and more innovative future. By embracing the principles of Infinite Potential Leadership—fostering growth, empowering others, and embracing innovation—leaders can not only drive transformational change but also unlock the full potential of their teams and organizations.

As we conclude this journey through Infinite Potential Leadership, it is time to shift from theory to action. The principles you have explored in this book—embracing continuous growth, empowering others, fostering innovation, building resilience, and leading with purpose—are not meant to remain abstract concepts. They are designed to be applied, lived, and integrated into every aspect of your life, both professionally and personally.

Leadership is not confined to the boardroom or the office. It is a way of being, a mindset that can transform not only how you lead others but also how you lead yourself. The essence of Infinite Potential Leadership is rooted in the belief that growth is boundless and that each of us has the capacity to unlock more potential than we ever imagined. This journey does not stop when you leave work at the end of the day. It continues in how you approach your personal challenges, relationships, and development.

The call to action is clear: take what you have learned and apply it in every area of your life. Whether you are leading a team through a challenging project, guiding a family member through a difficult time, or working to overcome your own personal obstacles, the principles of infinite potential remain the same. Commit to growth, embrace uncertainty, and believe in the limitless possibilities that lie within you and those around you.

Ask yourself, how can you become a better version of yourself tomorrow than you are today? What steps can you take to empower others in your life to achieve more than they think they are capable of? How can you create a ripple effect of growth and transformation in your personal and professional communities?

This is not just about climbing the career ladder or driving business success. It is about recognizing that the principles of leadership extend to every relationship and experience. Whether you are mentoring a colleague, raising children, or challenging yourself to achieve a personal goal, the mindset of infinite potential opens up a world of possibilities. So, take action. Begin with small steps and let them lead to larger transformations. Apply these principles with intention and watch how they expand your own capacity for growth, success, and fulfillment.

As you look to the future, one thing is certain—uncertainty is inevitable. But rather than seeing uncertainty as something to fear or avoid, recognize it for what it truly is: a space of infinite potential. The future is not fixed. It holds boundless possibilities, and the way you approach that future will determine how you unlock those opportunities. Leaders who embrace uncertainty with curiosity and resilience will thrive in times of change and shape the future with boldness and creativity.

Maintaining the mindset of infinite potential means continuously reminding yourself that your journey of growth is never complete. There will always be new challenges to face, new skills to develop, and new opportunities to pursue. It is easy to fall into the trap of thinking that you have reached your peak or that you have learned all there is to learn. However, true leaders, those who embody the principles of infinite potential, never stop evolving. They see each day as a new chance to grow, to innovate, and to push the boundaries of what is possible.

The uncertainty of the future is not something to be feared but embraced. It is a canvas of opportunity, a chance to redefine what is possible for yourself, your teams, and your organizations. As the world changes at an ever-increasing pace, leaders who remain adaptable, resilient, and committed to growth will not only navigate uncertainty—they will thrive in it.

So, as you move forward, carry with you these lessons. Embrace the unknown with confidence, knowing that you have the tools to turn challenges into opportunities and setbacks into stepping stones. Keep cultivating the mindset of infinite potential in yourself and in those around you. Trust that no matter what lies ahead, you can grow, lead, and transform in ways you may not yet even imagine.

The journey of leadership is long and winding, but it is also filled with promise and possibility. The future is unwritten, and you have the power to shape it. Embrace the mindset of infinite potential, and let it guide you toward a future of growth, impact, and endless opportunity. Lead with purpose, grow with intention, and always remember that your potential—and those around you—is truly unlimited.

This is your time. Take Infinite Potential Leadership, apply it in your life, and continue the journey of becoming the leader you are meant to be. The possibilities are infinite, and they are waiting for you.